Judging

By

Mere Mabery

Dedication

i

I dedicate this book, "Judging," to the loves of my life, my beloved sons, Jaleel D. Cole and Brakeem R. Jackson. Their support and endless love have been my guiding stars through every twist and turn of life's journey. Love You both to the moon and back, forever and always.

Acknowledgment

To my family, friends, and the exceptional team at US Ghost - writers, editors, proofreaders, logo designers, and website creators - your contributions have transformed this book into the masterpiece it is today, poised to inspire readers tomorrow.

Together, we have crafted something truly remarkable. Once again, I express my sincerest appreciation.

About the Author

Maryanne Mabery is the new captivating voice in the world of fiction (murder mystery), hailing from the city of Philadelphia, PA.

With an impressive background in finance spanning over two decades, Maryanne's journey from the world of numbers to the captivating realm of a murder mystery is as intriguing as the plots she expertly weaves.

Her journey began over ten years ago while working at an advertising agency, where she found herself captivated by the allure of storytelling through magazine articles. From that moment on, Maryanne's passion for writing blossomed, leading her to begin on a new creative path that would ultimately define her as an author.

In her debut book, ***"Judging,"*** Maryanne Mabery promises an enthralling experience that will keep readers eagerly turning pages, their minds brimming with suspense and anticipation. With a deft hand, she masterfully crafts a narrative that leaves readers both intrigued and a little confused, skillfully unraveling a mystery that keeps them guessing until the very end.

But beyond the twists and turns of the plot, Maryanne's writing reveals something deeper—her unique voice and perspective as a writer. Through her words, readers will glimpse into the soul of the author herself, discovering the essence of who Maryanne Mabery truly is.

Table of Contents

Page Left Blank Intentionally

Prologue

Welcome to the beautiful life of Kiara Tierson – A high profile judge

She's not a criminal, but…

She's not an addict, but…

She's not a failure, but…

She is tall, beautiful, and a smart woman. She's divorced – but it doesn't matter. She has two sons – Jason and Brent, and lives in a beautiful home in Miami. Perhaps this is all you need to know.

But everything changed when she met him – a man younger than her, yet possessing a magnetism that transcended age. His presence alone was enough to ignite a spark within her, a flicker of something long dormant, stirring to life with newfound intensity. Kiara doesn't care about the world. She calls it nothing but LOVE. But this love caused her great agony and suffering.

The best of her times turned into the worst of

her times. There were deep cuts – brutal deaths and bleeding hard. A war against blood splashed on the faces of everywhere.

They were watching her.

The monstrous lack of remorse.

Cold-blooded killers.

Something odd happened, and she fought back with buzzing energy. There is nothing so pitiful as to be betrayed by your loved ones.

No one knows what's happening until one day, the truth comes to life... and there is no judging!

Chapter 1
The Trial

MONDAY MORNING, 10:00 A.M.

•••

It began with the case of Mr. Romano, the most notorious drug cartel spanning across the United States and Mexico. His family owns a Yacht company and several commercial truck businesses to hide what they are doing in the US.

This case has been talked about many times before. But THIS time around, something has surfaced that is particularly tormenting for Carol.

Judge Carol Hidding's mind was working even faster now, probably too fast. So was her pulse. And she couldn't catch her breath either. She focused on the faces of the people instead, scanning for anything that might tell them why they were there.

The waiting was becoming excruciating, almost

impossible to bear. The spectators were quiet.

Something incredibly strange was going on; it was not all bad, necessarily, but it was strange. It was like no case she had ever worked or come across before.

As the proceedings began, the prosecutor presented a case outlining the extensive network of illegal activities orchestrated by the Romano family.

The prosecutor, Mr. David Anderson, stood up and whispered something, took a pause, and began questioning Mr. Romano. "So, you were not at the drug transportation place, Mr. Romano. Am I right?" "Yes sir, I wasn't," Romano said without any hesitation.

Judge Carol was silent. She seemed to be trying to get something clear to herself.

Attorney Winston Harper interrupted. "Objection, "Your Honor, I must object to the line of questioning. The question attempted to create a misleading narrative by asking the defendant about a specific location again and again without providing proper context."

While looking at Anderson, Carol said, "Objection noted. Proceed with caution, Counselor." Hidding's voice, once comfortable and reassuring, has now lost its warmth. It becomes a detached, unprofessional tone, leaving a subtle air of tension in the room.

Prosecutor David Anderson, leaning forward with a confident grin, "Your Honor, I appreciate the caution, but I assure you, I'm simply trying to establish a clear timeline of events."

Judge Carol Hidding, with a slight nod, remarked, "You may proceed now."

Anderson, undeterred, continues his questioning with a sly smile. He turned to the witness again, "So, Mr. Romano, you claim you weren't at the place of the alleged incident, right?"

"No, I wasn't there. I was at Starlight Sip Station, minding my own business. I have an alibi." Mr. Romano responded defensively.

Mr. David Anderson, with a smirk, proceeds, "An alibi? How convenient. Can anyone vouch for your whereabouts?"

Winston Harper stood up and interrupted, "Your Honor, I object again. The prosecutor is badgering the witness and insinuating guilt without proper evidence."

"Oh, so now we're supposed to take your word for it? No documents, no tangible proof. Your Honor, I request that the witness's claims be treated with skepticism until proper evidence is presented."

Judge Carol Hiddings, with a slight stern, said, "Sustained. Counselor, refrain from making baseless accusations. Stick to the facts."

"I... I don't have any documents, but the bar manager can confirm. We can ask him." Mr. Romano said.

Judge Carol Hiddings to Mr. Romano, "Since your alibi is centered around your presence at a particular bar during the time in question, I'd like to request calling the bar's manager to testify. Is that acceptable?"

"Yes, Your Honor. The manager can confirm I was there." Romano assured. "Very well. Court officer, please arrange for the bar's manager to be called to the stand." Judge Carol ordered.

(The court officer makes the necessary arrangements.)

The Bar's Manager, Mr. Josh Turner, took an oath and said, "I swear to tell the truth, the whole truth, and nothing but the truth."

"Mr. Romano claims he was at your bar during the time of the alleged incident. Can you confirm his presence?" Judge Carol inquired.

Mr. Josh Turner immediately responds, "Certainly, Your Honor. On the date in question, Mr. Romano was indeed at our establishment. He spent a considerable amount of time here.”

While raising an eyebrow, Carol asked, “And do you have any documentation or evidence to support this claim?”

“Yes, Your Honor. We maintain CCTV footage for security purposes. I can provide the relevant footage from that day, showing Mr. Romano at the bar during the hours he mentioned.”

“That evidence could be pivotal for the court’s deliberations. Kindly submit the footage to the court clerk for formal consideration,” Judge Carol said firmly.

(Mr. Josh hands over a USB drive containing the CCTV footage)

“Your Honor, I would like to review the footage before accepting it as evidence.” Attorney David Anderson requested.

“Certainly, Mr. Anderson, the court will adjourn briefly for you to examine the footage,” Carol replied.

(The court reviews the CCTV footage before the proceedings)

The courtroom tension rises as the cross-examination unfolds, leaving Mr. Romano’s fate hanging between being right and wrong.

Mr. David Anderson seemed determined not to give the defense at that moment. He backed up into his chair, settled himself, and regarded Winston Harper's evidence with haughty suspicion when confronted with a credible alibi.

Judge Carol Hidding returns to the courtroom after a 15-minute recess. The atmosphere is tense as everyone awaits her judgment.

While examining the courtroom, Judge Carol said, "Thank you all for your patience during the recess. I have carefully considered the evidence presented, and it is now time to render my judgment."

The room falls into a hushed silence as Judge Hidding takes a moment to gather her thoughts. Her eyes scanned the faces of those present, emphasizing the gravity of the decision about to be announced.

After a pause, Judge Carol Hidding said, "In the matter of Mr. Romano's case, after a thorough examination of the facts and testimony provided, this court decides to grant you three years' probation instead of jail time."

Everyone looked confusedly at the judge.

"But I want you to understand, Mr. Romano, that this decision is not a sign of leniency. But let me be very clear: if you violate the terms of your probation, there will be consequences. I expect that you will contribute positively to society." Judge Carol added.

"I won't let you down, Your Honor. I'm grateful for this opportunity." Mr. Romano said with a smirk.

This was it.

But it wasn't.

The courtroom clears as Judge Carol Hidding watches, silently hoping she made the right decision. But she wasn't happy or sad.

"I wasn't going any farther with Mr. Romano. All I could do was watch as he wheeled inside through the automatic sliders and out of sight. She had something on her mind. It wasn't just about the case being repeated; there was something else bothering her, something she wasn't saying. But that wasn't the bad part. The bad part was betraying Kiara. The clock kept ticking!" Judge Carol thought.

Judge Kiara Tierson wraps up her day, a sense of satisfaction evident on her face. She exits the courtroom, shedding the black judge gown for her street clothes, ready to leave for the day. Judge Kara Tieson is known for being very tough in the courtroom. She handles serious cases like drugs, murder, and robbery. Even for smaller crimes, she often gives long sentences, like thirty years, which can seem too much. Some people don't like her for that, but others love and respect her.

On the other hand, her friend and colleague, Judge Carol Hidding, is different. She is not as strict as Kiara. Carol believes in giving people more chances, even if they make mistakes.

This difference in their approaches makes their friendship a bit shaky because Kiara wants Carol to be tougher like her.

As Judge Kiara walks towards the parking lot, Mr. Romano spots her. Unaware of her judicial role, he approaches her with a confident smile.

With a smirk, Mr. Romano said, "Hey there, beautiful. Fancy seeing someone as stunning as you around here."

Judge Kiara, maintaining her composure, gives him a polite smile but continues walking without responding to his advances.

Mr. Romano, undeterred, walks alongside her,

trying to engage in conversation. "I will have you one day, my love, sooner than later." Judge Kiara looks back at him, her expression unwavering, yet a hint of annoyance flickers in her eyes. She remains silent, refusing to acknowledge his comment.

As Mr. Romano exits the building, Judge Kiara watches him leave with a steely gaze. Unfazed by the encounter, she waits for Judge Hidding, determined to discuss the case's outcome. However, Judge Hidding swiftly leaves the building, avoiding any interaction with Kiara, who is both her boss and friend.

Undeterred, Judge Kiara decides to take matters into her own hands. She heads home and promptly calls her colleague and friend, DA McBrow.

"Hello, hi, it's Kiara."

"I know who you are, Judge Kiara. What's up?" DA McBrow replied.

"Well, that's great."

"Listen, I need to ask you about an upcoming case. I'll give you the details, but I won't mention any names. Just want your opinion on something that Judge Carol and I were discussing." "Sure thing, Kiara. Shoot."

Kiara poses thought-provoking questions,

carefully avoiding any direct mention of names or specifics.

Da Mcbrow, while taking it all in, finally said, "You're asking some pretty intense questions. What's really going on, Kiara?"

Reassuring Judge Kiara responds, "Yeah, everything is okay. Just wanted to get your opinion on the matter, McBrow. What do you think about the situation?"

As the conversation unfolds, DA McBrow becomes increasingly skeptical about the nature of Judge Kiara's inquiries. Sensing his suspicion, Kiara quickly kept on reassuring him.

"Thanks for your input. I'll catch up with you later."

She hangs up, leaving DA McBrow with lingering questions. Meanwhile, Judge Kiara contemplates the shared insights, turning her thoughts toward the enigmatic nature of the case and the complexity of her relationship with Judge Carol.

Judge Kiara dials Judge Carol Hidding's number, but there's no answer. Instead, Judge Carol's husband, Dan, picks up the phone.

"Hello, Dan. It's Kiara. Is Carol around?"

"Oh, hey, Kiara. Carol's actually in the bath right

now. Can I give her a message?"

"Sure, Dan. Please tell her to call me before the night ends. If not tonight, then ask her to stop by my office around 9:30 am tomorrow, okay?"

"I'll let her know, Kiara. Take care."

After hanging up the phone, Judge Kiara senses that something might be amiss. She contemplates the situation, feeling an undercurrent of unease. Determined to get to the bottom of things, she gets into her bed and decides to find out more tomorrow.

The next day arrives, and there's no sign of Judge Carol. Kiara, increasingly concerned, begins to investigate, trying to unravel the mystery behind Carol's sudden absence. The day unfolds with unanswered questions, leaving Kiara on edge as she searches for clues to explain the unexpected turn of events.

Two weeks passed, and Carol continued to avoid Kiara, her boss and friend. The silence between them grows, leaving Kiara increasingly upset.

Finally, Kiara manages to catch up with Carol in her courtroom during an ongoing trial. As Kiara quietly slips into a seat, Judge Carol Hidding visibly becomes nervous, her composure faltering as she notices Kiara's presence.

During a one-hour recess called by Judge Carol Hidding, Judge Kiara approaches her with urgency.

"Carol, we need to talk."

"Kiara, can't it wait? I'm in the middle of a trial."

"No, it can't wait. This is important." Kiara responded with a sense of urgency.

They step into a quieter corner of the courthouse, away from prying ears.

Judge Carol Hidding, with an irritation, responded, "What's so urgent?"

"It's about Romano. I told you to give him at least ten years, and you gave him another chance?"

Judge Carol Hidding responds defensively, "Kiara, I know what I'm doing. Not every case is black and white."

She raised her voice, "But Carol, he's a repeat offender! He doesn't deserve another chance."

"I promised I would handle it. Can't you trust me?" Judge Carol answered with frustration.

"I trusted you, Carol. But this is about justice, not personal promises."

"Kiara, not everything is about following your

strict rules!”

“Sometimes, it’s about doing what’s right! Romano deserves to pay for his crimes.”

“Fine! Handle it your way!” Kiara storms off, leaving Carol frustrated and alone.

BACK THEN – THURSDAY MORNING

●●●

On Thursday morning, Kiara and Carol met for coffee to discuss a case.

“Good morning, Kiara.” “Good morning, Carol. How are you?” “Good. Listen, Kiara, I need to talk to you about a case I’m working on.” “Okay, Carol. I’m all ears.” “Kiara, you’re my best friend and boss. I need your opinion on this case.”

Kiara nodded and said, “Sure, Carol. I’m here for you. What’s going on with this case?” After a long pause, Carol exhaled and said, “I have this case coming before me next week, and I’m very confused about how it should go.”

“Alright, Carol. What’s the case about, and what’s confusing?” Kiara asked sincerely.

“Well, he keeps getting locked up for the same

stuff, and I'm tired of giving him a chance after chance after chance. I want to give him ten years for repeat offenses."

"Okay, Carol. Give him ten years and be done with it. Close the case and move on to the next one."

"Carol, what's so hard about that? Now, I'm confused about why you're not suggesting ten to twenty at the most."

"I want to throw the book at this guy. It's complicated and hard to explain, but I must give him one more chance to get his life back on track and hopefully become a better person in society."

"Give me a little about the case. I must go; I have two meetings in 20 minutes."

Carol Hidding sighs, "He sells weight, and I keep giving him a second, third, and fourth chance to get it together. I'm tired as hell of this loser and his family."
"What does his family have to do with this case? Hell with his family, and do the right thing."

"Kiara, he's young, 33 years old. He knows right from wrong, and I say give it to him."

"It's not his fault. Whose fault is it, Kiara? He had no guidance or anything."

"Carol, it's his character, and he has no control over it. Keep me posted on this case, and if you need help, let me know. I would love this case. How about a case transfer? That would help."

"No, I got it. I got it. When he gets out, I bet he will turn his life around and become a better person."

"He's been in and out of jail all his life," Carol replied.

"Carol, if you keep giving him a chance after chance, he's going to kill someone, and that's on your head."

"Thanks, Kiara."

"Don't forget to keep me posted on this, and remember ten to twenty years. I bet he gets his life together sitting and thinking for a very long time."

The divergence in philosophies between Kiara and Carol becomes starkly evident. Kiara, unswayed by the fear that holds Carol, views justice as a means of doing society a favor, getting rid of what she labels as "losers." She doesn't seek to know their names; she desires results.

"Goodbye, I must call you later," Kiara announces, leaving the courtroom with a determined stride.

Meanwhile, Carol, left alone in her contemplation, sits with the weight of an impending decision on her shoulders.

In the solitude of her thoughts, Carol is grappled with the dilemma before her. She closed her eyes and took several deep, long breaths, preparing for the hard road that lay ahead. She wanted to stay at home and have a normal life, but there was no going back.

She took a breath, feeling more frustrated than sympathetic, and left the place.

Chapter 2
The Meet-Up

Tuesday Midnight: 2:00 a.m.

•••

Carol jolted from a deep slumber in the middle of the night, and the room is dark, the air close, and sweet. It's different, though. She began looking straight through the window.

Dan wasn't at home; he had a night shift at work. The usual comfort of his presence was absent. Carol tiptoed to check on her sleeping children. Everything seemed okay.

Returning to her room, Carol found herself standing before the window again.

Is someone looking at me?

I could feel someone's eyes on me.

Who was watching me?

The night had an eerie stillness. There was no

moon, just darkness everywhere.

She heard someone scratching in the backyard. As she got to the main hallway, the noise felt a crushing sensation of wrongness, shame, and betrayal. She didn't feel like herself—the way she used to be.

She stepped out of the house and followed the whisper. A feeling of unease gripped her as she approached the mysterious noise. But the voice was gone when Carol got there.

"Hello?" Carol's voice quivered as she called out into the darkness.

"Is someone there? I heard scratching. Is anyone out here?"

Carol stood in the solitude of her backyard, the weight of the silence pressing upon her. A barely discernible murmur brushed against the darkness of the air as she began walking.

There were no clear words, just an enigma.

As she tried looking back, Carol stumbled on uneven ground, and before she could react, she found herself falling to the cold, damp earth. Her hands were bloodstained—if you kill someone, you could never wash the blood off.

She closed her eyes; her body felt like folding into tiny bits of pieces.

She was frightened and wanted to disappear.

"Help me!"

For an instant, she felt dead.

Carol hastily rose from her position and sprinted toward her house, her hand smeared with blood. As she entered — a shattered mirror lay broken on the floor.

Carol ran to her kids' room, gasping. She entered and found her children sleeping comfortably. Carol cried hysterically.

She could feel the heat on her face, her stomach a pit of acid. A few days ago—a sensible, clearheaded, and right-thinking woman—she decided that her part in this story is smooth no more but chaotic.

She stood in the shower, gradually reducing the water temperature, making it hot until it was properly warm. The warm water soothed her skin; it wiped out the bloodstain from her hands.

She took a laptop downstairs and made a cup of tea. There's a chance, a faint one, that she decided to write an email to Kiara. She took a deep breath, opened her Gmail account, and was relieved to see no messages. She wrote an email to Kiara but didn't send it. She clicked on the message again and read it twice:

Could you please help me? I'm feeling pretty low, don't you think? I'm trying to get out of trouble, but I can't. You could be in real trouble. I have done something very miserable.

She closed her eyes and snapped the laptop shut. She was frightened and sat in complete silence.

I don't understand the person I've become. Kiara and Dan would hate me. I hate myself, too – the real version of myself is dead. I'm not hateful, but I'm stupid. Carol thought.

The next morning, Dan came back home, he looked at Carol with concern as they sat across from each other in the dimly lit kitchen. He could sense something was amiss.

"You slept last night," Dan inquired gently, his brow furrowed in concern.

"No, and Yes," Carol replied without looking at Dan.

"What does that mean?" Dan observed that something wasn't right.

"I don't know."

"Is everything okay? You look upset," Dan asked with genuine worry.

Carol sighed, "I heard something in the backyard."

Dan leaned forward, "What was that?"

"I don't know, it was a scratching sound, and when I went to check, there was nothing there. Just darkness and silence."

"Wonder what it looks like?" Dan asked her.

"I…I don't know." Carol mumbled.

"Maybe it was just an animal or the wind, sweetheart. You know how these things can play tricks on your mind." Dan said.

Carol nodded, "I hope so. It just felt... unsettling, you know?"

"We can check together tonight if it makes you feel better. I'm sure it's nothing to worry about." He assured her while bending down to kiss her head.

WEEKS LATER….

•••

Days turned into weeks, and there was still an uneasy silence between the once-called best friends — Judge Carol and Kiara.

Weeks ago almost two to three weeks ago, Carol walked out of our friendship. Carol is not a mystery to be solved or a character that comes into a film's opening tracking shot, gorgeous, ethereal, and insubstantial. She's not a cipher. She's real. Kiara thought.

Okay, that's enough now!!!

Kiara dialed her number, not knowing how she would react. She spoke to her in a low voice, as though there was someone else in the room, someone he didn't want to overhear. "Can we talk in person?" Kiara asked. "I . . . no. I don't think so . . ." Carol said abruptly.

"Please?"

Carol hesitated just for a moment and then agreed. "Okay, fine."

"Could you come to the Bean Bliss coffee house this evening?"

"Okay, I'll be there at 4:00 p.m.," Carol responded.

After hanging up the call, Kiara started thinking about her now. She had to convince Carol to tell her everything—a little, not a lot.

I think about her as my real friend: funny, beautiful, caring, and warmhearted. Kiara pondered.

She needed to cool down, to get things straight in

her head. She thought about all the arguments they both had and all the terrible things they did to each other.

Kiara left the courthouse and drove to the coffee house. She felt quite befuddled while driving.

Once reached, she approached the corner table where Judge Carol Hidding was already seated. As Kiara drew closer to Carol, their eyes met, exchanging a silent acknowledgment of the strained situation they were stuck in.

"Look, Carol, I know you have been avoiding me for weeks, and I know there's something not okay with you. "We are friends, and I'm worried about you," Kiara said.

"There's nothing wrong, and you don't have to get worried about me," Carol said coldly.

"What about that case? We need to discuss the case and find a resolution. It's our duty as judges to ensure justice is served."

Judge Carol Hidding sighed, realizing the severity of the situation. "Kiara, I had my reasons for giving him another chance."

Judge Kiara's eyes narrowed, "Carol, this is not about personal feelings or hidden agendas. You know what I mean here, right? We have a responsibility to uphold the law and deliver justice. If you have valid reasons for your decision, you need to share them with me. We can't have different interpretations of the law affecting our judgments."

Carol folded her arms and leaned back, her expression defiant. "Kiara, not every decision needs to be dissected and analyzed. I can have my reasons, and I don't owe you an explanation for every choice I make. I'll handle the consequences of my decisions. You focus on your cases, and I'll focus on mine. We don't need to agree on everything."

"Don't you dare for one second forget who I am, your boss, and I need answers about that case we talked about, Judge Carol Hidding. We have one hour to talk about it."

Judge Carol, seeming defensive, responded, "I had to give him another chance, Kiara. That's it!"

Kiara's frustration boiled over at Carol's response. "What the hell did you just say to me? Give that bum another chance when I told you to give him at least ten years behind bars so he could think about his life."

"Kiara, you don't understand; there's more to it,"

Carol pleaded.

"Okay, what's the more to it? Explain now, Judge Carol Hidding. Right Now! Don't play with me, damn it! I will take care of it." Judge Kiara demanded an explanation.

Carol attempted to reassure her, "No, I will handle it."

"No, Judge Hidding, you should have taken care of it already. You are soft and should have never been a judge—maybe a low life."

"Judge Kiara, you climbed your way to the top by using your relationships. I'm not like you."

"Oh, right, you're not like me. You are a screw-up, and you can't do your job right," Kiara shot back angrily.

"I like to give people second and third chances, not like you, Judge Kiara. You give young men and young women 30 years when you should have given them 6 or 7 years. You are miserable!!!"

"Look, who's saying this, the one who is a miserable judge? You don't know if I fuck my way to the top." Kiara responded.

"You did Judge Kiara. Did you forget that you had sex with congressmen, professors, and so many more?

You are a whore with two amazing sons, and they don't know who their father is." Carol remarked aggressively.

"And what did you have? A corny Dan Hidding?" He made you a cornball."

"FUCK YOU KIARA! FUCK YOU!!!"

"You Bit*ch!!!!" Carol yelled loudly.

The people around them couldn't help but notice the argument going on between them. Whispers and curious glances circulated among the onlookers, creating a hushed buzz in the atmosphere.

"I'm going to write you up and take over that case. As I walk away, you can pucker your lips and look down, and you know the rest." Judge Kiara said with a menacing smile.

Judge Hidding, feeling cornered, continued to yell in fear for her family. The stakes were high, and the threat of Judge Kiara taking over the case seemed to have dire consequences.

Things have started turning into worse!

What should I do?

There will be blood everywhere!

Times goes on….. The clock is ticking!!!

Judge Kiara starts the process of getting Judge

Hidding to kick off this case, and she will take this case into her own hands. I don't lose. She should know this about me. I don't lose games like this. If she thinks I'm going to sit around crying over her, she's got another thing coming. I can do everything without her just fine—but I don't like to lose. It's not like me. None of this is like me. I don't get rejected. I'm the one who walks away.

The tension between Judge Carol Hidding and Judge Kiara Tierson had reached a boiling point, and their meetings only intensified the conflict more and more.

Carol and Kiara met once again, but this time in Kiara's office, attempting to resolve the issues that had strained their relationship.

The same argument – Every time!!!

"Why are you so uptight about this case, Judge Hiding? You need to tell me what's going on. Are you involved with him?" Judge Kiara questioned, giving her a nasty look.

"I'm not like you, Judge Kiara. I have told you this many times."

"You have one week to get me all I need, or I will reopen that case and take care of it the right way. Leave this alone, or I'm going to your boss."

Judge Carol, feeling attacked, yelled back, "You're just jealous of my life! I'm married to a great man, unlike you. You don't even know who the father of your child is since you have been involved with so many different men at the same time."

Carol left her office, pushing people in the hallway out of her way, crying, and walking fast. She was in a state of distress and, feeling overwhelmed, contemplated her options as she desperately sought a way to reach Judge Kiara's boss before it was too late. Tears streamed down her face, and the weight of the situation bore down on her.

After a few hours, Kiara called Judge Carol and issued a fierce warning again. "If you call my boss, I'll be that lion that will tear your ass up. Don't play with me, Judge Carol Hidding. You don't know me."

Faced with this new threat, Judge Carol hung up the call immediately. She is fearful and confused.

No matter how much trouble Kiara causes, I have to be strong. Carol said to herself while sobbing.

She did wash up, tidying up the living room, and thinking about dinner. Something easy and light. She used to hate the thought of staying in and cooking, but now she finds it great to be her family.

To forget whatever is happening!

To run away from all the worries!

To get the normal life that she had before the case!

But there's nothing more to do.

EVENING

•••

Kiara felt dreadful. She just didn't know what she had to be afraid of. But she wanted to be with someone. So, she called her childhood friend Michelle.

"Hello," Kiara said.

"Hi Kiara, What's up?"

"Hi Michelle"

"I really need to talk to you, okay?"

"Yeah, sure, but are you okay?" Michelle asked with concern.

Kiara quickly dismissed any worries, "Yeah, all good. Let's meet for dinner, just you. I wanted to see you."

"I'll get Shannon to pick up Zana, and I'll meet you around 6:00 p.m. at Velvet Olive restaurant, okay? I really hope you meet your future husband there." Michelle chuckled.

"Okay, see you, girl. Bye," Kiara said and hung up the call.

There was a rush of elation and uneasiness, but Kiara stood up to get ready. She washed her hair and put some makeup on. She wore a black velvet shirt and jeans and low-heeled sandals.

I look OK. She kept telling herself while standing in front of the mirror.

As the sun dipped below the horizon, Judge Kiara headed out to meet Michelle for dinner. The city lights began to twinkle, and people gathered in restaurants, parks, and squares.

Kiara and Michelle settled into their seats; Michelle couldn't help but bring up the idea of romance, "Kiara, who knows? Maybe tonight's the night you meet someone special."

Judge Kiara chuckled, "Oh, really, we'll see."

As they engaged in conversation, a familiar presence emerged in the periphery. From across the room, Mr. Romano was staring at Kiara. He was captivated by her beauty and charm.

"Hi, my name is Romano," he said.

Kiara looked at him. He was dressed in a charcoal gray

jacket that accentuated his well-defined frame. The crisp white shirt beneath the jacket looked perfect. His neatly combed hair added a polished appearance to his face. He looked handsome and a well-groomed man.

Despite Romano's undeniable handsomeness, Kiara expressed her disinterest.

"Not interested," she said.

"Fair enough, I respect that. If you ever change your mind, I'll be around. Have a great evening." Mr. Romano responded and left.

Michelle nudged Kiara, "Come on, Kara, talk to him."

Kiara smirked, "No, he looks like... you know."

"You haven't been with a man in three years. I'm sick and tired of hearing about Brent's father cheating on you for a younger girl. Forget about Brent's father now. Give someone else a chance. This man looks handsome."

"No, I came here to meet and talk to you, not to meet someone else, Michelle," Kiara asserted.

"Come on, Kiara, a little conversation won't hurt. Who knows, it might be a nice distraction." Michelle persisted.

Kiara, trying to keep things light, responded, "Again, Not interested, girl."

"Okay, let's talk about Judge Carol. What happened

between you two?" Michelle changed the topic.

Kiara recounted the hurtful words Carol had thrown at her—calling her a whore and accusing her of climbing the career ladder by sleeping with men.

"What!!! She called you a whore and said you fuck your way to the top, and you don't know who Jason's father is. Wow! That's not a friend; that sounds like an enemy," Michelle remarked.

"You know who Jason's father is. He's still married and took great care of Jason financially. He didn't spend much time with Jason, but financially, he was a great provider." Michelle continued.

"I know."

"So, what did you say?" Michelle asked.

A mischievous smile played on Kiara's lips. "I called her husband corny."

"Well, he is very corny," Michelle agreed, and they both burst into laughter.

The two friends shared a few more anecdotes, finding comfort in each other's company. But Kiara had to leave.

"I have to get home. I have five cases tomorrow, and I need to get to the courthouse early," Kiara said with a determined tone.

"Yeah, sure, okay, bye. Love you, girl," Michelle said smilingly.

"We will meet again. I love you more," Kiara replied while leaving the restaurant.

She made her way to the car park after having a great dinner with Michelle. While walking to her car, she found herself unexpectedly accompanied by Mr. Romano. He followed her to the parking lot.

"Hey, what's wrong? Are you following me?" Kiara asked concernedly.

"Nothing's wrong. Nothing at all. Following you didn't mean anything, of course." Mr. Romano answered while looking at her, waiting and expectant.

Kiara could see the muscle flex in his jaw as he clenched his teeth.

"Leave me alone," Kiara firmly said.

"Can't we be just friends?" Mr. Romano replied.

"I don't make friends with strangers." Kiara retorted.

"But we can be if you will give it a chance."

"And may I know the good reason for giving you a chance?" Kiara said, looking into his eyes.

Mr. Romano took a deep breath and said, "Umm… I…I don't know, but we will be good friends, trust me. A friend in need is a friend indeed."

"Not at this stage," she said. "But thank you."

He was talking to her like someone she could trust—
and she knew that it was wrong, but it felt so good to her
after a long time.

Romano, flashing a charming smile, said, "Hey, Kiara,
I've really enjoyed our conversation. How about we stay
in touch? Can I get your number?"

"I'm not really into giving my number to strangers,"
Kiara said with a smirk.

"Ah, I completely understand. But what if we became
friends? Just friends were sharing a few laughs and stories.
What do you say?"

"I don't usually make friends easily."

Romano, with a playful tone, added, "Well, maybe we
can break that pattern. Let me prove that I can be a good
friend. What harm could it do?"

"Okay, fine. Here's my number. But don't expect too
much."

"I appreciate the chance, Kiara. I promise I'll be a good
friend. I won't disappoint you."

"Well, that's great, bye."

"I should go now, too," he said. "I've taken up enough

of your time. Take care, see you soon!"

TUESDAY MORNING, 11:00 A.M.

●●●

The next morning, as the sun painted the sky with hues of orange and pink, Mr. Romano decided to reach out to Kiara. He dialed her number, hoping to extend their connection from the previous night.

"Hi, Kiara! I hope you remember me. How about lunch today?" Romano suggested enthusiastically.

"Hey, stranger, What's up? I appreciate the offer, but I'm swamped with work today. I can't take some time for myself," she explained.

"Are you sure? A quick lunch break could do wonders. Just a friendly meal, no strings attached." Mr. Romano tried to persuade her.

Kiara hesitated, "I appreciate the offer, really. But my mind is elsewhere right now," she replied with a sigh.

"No worries, Kiara. Whenever you're ready, just let me know. I'm here."

"Okay, Bye!"

They both hung up the call immediately.

Kiara spent the whole day going through Carol's things

again and again. She was looking out for something, anything that would give her an indication as to where she could be at the moment and what she could be hiding for a very long time.

But there's nothing. No emails, no letters, no calls, nothing. Kiara thought about trying to contact her.

Is that a good idea? I don't know, I just don't know. She had no comfort without knowing the truth. I don't want to say it out loud, but we must both be thinking that there's something dangerous. Kiara asked herself.

Chapter 3
Uninvited Agony

•••

Rung! Rung!

Carol's phone rang. He hurried and picked up the call.

It was an unknown number. With a gentle breath, she picked up the receiver. "Hello?" she greeted.

On the other end of the line, a voice belonging to a man who called himself UNC spoke, "You might not know me now, but you will if my nephew doesn't come home tomorrow," he warned cryptically.

A frown creased Carol's forehead. "I'm sorry, but I don't know you," she replied cautiously.

The man's tone turned ominous. "You'll get to know me really well, especially if Judge Hidding doesn't rule in favor of my nephew tomorrow."

"So, do you know who I am?" Carol questioned confidently.

The man on the phone chuckled darkly. "I know more than you think. You are the judge, and if you do not make the right decision, then you might find your husband and children in a perilous situation. Let me spell it out for you – DEAD."

Carol choked for a while, and her eyes widened with fear and anxiety. However, she held herself with courage and responded, "Who the hell do you think you are, threatening a federal judge and her family? This is a serious case, and I will have you arrested!"

A sinister chuckle resonated through the phone. "No, Judge Hidding, you won't because you don't know who the hell I am. You'll get to know me very well if you don't release my nephew tomorrow. I run this town, the police station, the mayor, the governor, and, oh yeah, the President of the United States."

Carol's disbelief was palpable. "You can't possibly control all of that, so may I know who are you really?"

The voice on the other end turned serious and grave. "You will find out soon enough. Just remember, your husband and kids are in my sights. Make the right decision, Judge, or face the consequences."

As the line went silent, Carol was left grappling with the gravity of the situation. The stakes were higher than she could have ever imagined.

The man on the phone continued, "Let's make the right decision pertaining to Mr. Romano tomorrow. Got a big party planned – you and the family are welcome."

Despite the forced invitation, the man's tone held a menacing edge. "Let's not forget, final warning, Judge Carol Hidding. I don't like repeating myself. Oh yeah, I'm not asking you; I'm telling you – release Mr. Romano tomorrow. Is that understood, Judge Hidding?"

An uneasy silence followed, broken only by Carol's hesitant reply, "Yes, understood."

With that, the mysterious caller hung up, leaving Judge Hidding staring at the phone in her trembling hands. Fear gripped her, and her thoughts spiraled into chaos. What should I do? What should I do? she muttered to herself, looking out for answers.

She was left with no choice!

She cried. My family, my career!

I... I.... I can't let this happen!

I will find a way out!

●●●

Every night, Judge Carol had scary dreams that made her feel depressed and upset. These nightmares were like a never-ending loop, bringing back bad memories and making her feel trapped in fear and uncertainty about the future.

As the nights went on, these bad dreams got worse, and Carol felt more and more vulnerable. She couldn't escape from the scary thoughts haunting her mind. The nightmares made her doubt if she was safe in her own house and even made her question if she was losing her mind.

Dan noticed Carol's distant expression as they conversed. Concerned, he gently interrupted their usual exchange, stopping in his tracks and furrowing his brow. "Are you all right?" he asked, a genuine worry etched on his face. "You look... kind of out of it."

"I'm just a bit tired," Carol answered him. "I'm not feeling very well. I think I'll go to bed."

"Take care, Carol. If you ever need someone to talk to,

I'm here."

As Carol retreated to her space, Dan couldn't help but wonder about the struggles she was facing with the cases. He knew that Carol had been going through something, but she wasn't ready to share it with anyone else.

FRIDAY EVENING

•••

Kiara was sitting on the sofa in her living room, a glass of wine in her hand. It was dark and a bit cold outside.

While thinking about the cases, out of nowhere, her mind drifted to Mr. Romano, who called her previously.

She found herself contemplating the image of his presence—his countenance and the cadence of his speech.

Kiara stared at her phone, lost in her thoughts about Mr. Romano, when suddenly she got an incoming call from him.

Oh my God, does he know that I wanted to talk to him?
Does he know that I was thinking about him?
Oh my God......!

"Hello?" she greeted tentatively.

"Kiara," he said smoothly. "You were thinking about

me, weren't you?"

There was a momentary silence as Kiara processed the unexpected connection. "Well, yes and no. I… I mean, no, I wasn't."

"Really?"

"Yeah, I wasn't. I was thinking about something else, and you crossed my mind."

"Sometimes, the universe nudges us to revisit memories and reconnect." He said with a soft chuckle.

Kiara smiled, "Ah, really. So, what made you call now The Universe?"

"I was actually missing you and wanted to see you," he said, with warmth in his voice, "I've enjoyed our conversation. Would you be open to meeting? Please don't say no."

"I…I'm busy." She said, trying to avoid the meet-up.

"Please." He whispered.

"Umm….Okay."

"Great, so how about we have dinner this weekend?" Let's say Saturday around 8:00 p.m. at the Coastal Suite?" he suggested.

"Sounds great," she agreed.

"Perfect. I'll see you then."

Finally, after all this time, I'm going to do it with none other than Mr. Romano, who was in her mind.

SATURDAY

•••

On Saturday, Kiara woke up in the morning with a sense of anticipation and excitement bubbling within her. The prospect of meeting Mr. Romano filled her thoughts with curiosity and wonder. As she went through her morning routine, she felt happy while being with a man after a long time.

As the evening came, she arrived at the meeting spot, and there it was – The Coastal Suite.

Kiara gave her car keys to the valet and made her way to the building. To her surprise, Mr. Romano was already seated at a table, a view of the ocean stretching beyond the windows behind him.

He was dressed in his white linen shirt and black pants. He looked heart-stoppingly handsome. His dark copper hair was messed up, giving a casual charm.

Wow! Kiara said to herself while walking towards him.

As she approached him, they exchanged warm smiles, and they greeted each other.

"Mr. Romano, it's a pleasure to see you. I hope you didn't wait too long."

Mr. Romano stood up and nodded gently. "Not at all, Kiara. The pleasure is mine. Please, have a seat."

Kiara took a seat opposite him, "This coastal suite is breathtaking. You picked a wonderful spot."

"But to me, you look absolutely breathtaking tonight. That emerald dress suits you perfectly."

Kiara was wearing a beautiful emerald satin dress that gracefully complemented her figure. Her hair was meticulously tied in a messy bun, completing the polished and refined look for the dinner date.

Kiara, appreciative of the compliment, responded with a gracious smile.

"Let's start the evening with some champagne and caviar, shall we?" Mr. Romano said.

Kiara was delighted by the suggestion and nodded in agreement.

The waiter promptly brought over a chilled bottle of champagne and a great selection of caviar.

Mr. Romano raised his glass, "To shared moments and new beginnings."

Kiara joined in, clinking her glass against his. "To

shared moments and new beginnings." She responded.

After enjoying the sparkling champagne and savoring the delicacy of caviar, they continued their evening with dinner.

Mr. Romano was sitting in front of her, and she had an unprecedented opportunity to study him. His lovely face looks younger.

How could anyone look this good?

It would be tempting to reach out and touch him, but like a small baby.

"You know, I like having you here with me." He frowned as he said this and then glanced at his watch. "It's not late." And he turns to look at her. "You're biting your lip. Does that mean something?" His voice becomes a bit husky.

Kiara gasped… how can he say things like that to me and not expect me to be affected?

"Kiara, before you head home, would you mind staying a bit longer? I make a great cup of coffee." Mr. Romano asked.

"A cup of your great coffee, huh? Well, I suppose I can spare a few more minutes. Lead the way." She said with a wide smile on her face.

She felt happy around him.

She wanted to stay close to him.

Once inside his hotel room, she saw a beautiful and vast bedroom. The walls were white, and the furnishings were pale blue and gray. While she was looking around, Mr. Romano began making coffee for her.

As he finished preparing the coffee, he handed a steaming cup to Kiara with a genuine smile. "Here you go."

"Wow, this is really good! You weren't kidding about your coffee-making skills."

Mr. Romano grinned, pleased with the reaction. "I'm glad you like it. It's amazing what a good cup of coffee can do—brings people together, doesn't it?"

"Really?"

"Yes, it does."

As they sat together, enjoying their coffee, Kiara's curiosity got the better of her. "If you don't mind me asking, tell me about your family. Do you have any siblings or close relatives?"

His expression changed slightly, "Actually, Kiara, I live alone. I don't have anyone in my family."

"I'm really sorry. I shouldn't have asked you this."

Kiara responded apologetically.

"My parents... they passed away in a car accident when I was quite young. I never had any siblings, just an aunt who took me in and raised me."

"I'm so sorry to hear that."

"Huh, that's okay. You know, Kiara, as time passed, life led me on a different journey, and now I find myself living independently."

"It must have been a difficult journey. I can only imagine the strength it took to navigate through such experiences."

Mr. Romano smiled faintly. "Life has its way of shaping us, doesn't it? Each experience, every twist and turn, contributes to who we are today."

She wrapped her arms around his shoulders, bringing them into a closer embrace. Caught in the heat of the moment, their lips met in a spontaneous and passionate kiss. Time seemed to stand still as the world around them faded away, leaving only the shared intensity of the tender kiss.

The warmth of the connection they had been building throughout the evening now took on a more intimate and profound dimension.

As they pulled away, their eyes locked. Feeling the magnetic pull between them, Mr. Romano couldn't resist the undeniable connection that had ignited with their first kiss. Without hesitation, they found themselves locked in another kiss.

"You smell so good, So sweet." His nose skims past her ear down her neck, and he trails soft, featherlight kisses along her shoulder.

Oh ... no, what will this mean?

"Come," he murmured, gazing at her.

"Where?" Kiara asked.

"I want you." Mr. Romano said.

"You want what?" she asked.

"I want you. "I can't keep still if you're going to bite that lip," he warned her.

Holy hell, He's asking me to sleep with him.

What am I going to do? He knows everything.

He lifted her up and took her to the bedroom. She flushed and blinked at the same time.

It's so frustrating—I am desperate to do it.

Did I come here to sleep with him? Really?

Her breath became shallow, and she couldn't take her eyes off him. He removes his watch and places it on top of a chest of drawers that matches the bed, and removes his jacket, placing it neatly on a chair.

He opened the top drawer of the chest and removed a packet of condoms while gazing at me.

Oh, Holy Hell.

He walked towards her slowly. Condent, sexy, eyes flaming, and her heart starts to race. He looked down into her eyes.

He's insanely hot.

"Do you have any idea how much I want you," he whispered. Her breath hitched. He reached up and gently ran his fingers down her cheek. "Do you have any idea what I'm going to do to you with you, Kiara?" he said while caressing her chin.

Leaning down, he kissed her passionately. His lips were demanding, slow at times, soft while molding her lips.

He started unbuttoning her dress while he kissed her cheeks, chin, and jaw. He stood up and stared at her, and she was in a perfect lacy red bra.

His hands move beneath the waistband, skimming her and moving to her behind. His hands glide slowly down her backside to her thighs, removing her red panties and throwing them away.

They were gone. Thank heavens!

"You have the most beautiful skin. It's pale and sexy. I want every inch of it. I want every inch of you right here, right now."

Now I'm lying naked in front of a man. He's naked, too.

He grasped her hair tie and pulled it free, down around her shoulders. He kissed her again.

Ah! I moaned.

He put his arms around her and hauled her against his body, squeezing her tightly yet gently.

His one hand is still in her hair, while the other moves down her spine, waist, and down to her behind.

They both breathe… too loud breathing this time.

They both moaned.

"Keep yourself still." He demanded.

After the passionate love-making, he gazed down at her with a satisfied smile on his face.

That was extraordinary.

They both felt not too hot, not too cold. Leaning down, he tenderly kissed her lips, and his weight shifted on the bed, and they went to sleep in each other's arms.

In the morning, Kiara stirred from her slumber, the

soft morning light filtering through the curtains. As she opened her eyes, she realized the bed was empty, and a faint sense of confusion washed over her. Mr. Romano was nowhere to be found.

"Where could he be?"

He was nowhere to be found. The breakfast was made and kept on the kitchen table. A shirt and a pair of jeans were placed nearby, carefully laid out for her.

She glanced around the room, trying to recall the details of how she ended up there. The memories of the dinner, the coffee, and the passionate kisses and sex flooded back into her mind.

She reached for her phone and attempted to call Mr. Romano but his number appeared unreachable. Kiara furrowed her brow, wondering if there might be some technical glitch or if he was in an area with poor reception. She tried again, but the result was the same — no answer.

Taking a moment to collect herself, Kiara took a bath, wore a shirt and jeans, and got ready to leave for home. Mr. Romano was still nowhere to be found. No messages and no calls!!!

Kiara, still carrying the memories of the intriguing night with Mr. Romano, arrived home with a heart full of emotions.

"Hey, Brent, how was your day?" Kiara asked.

Brent looked up, his face lighting up at the sight of his mother. "Mom! It was good. I worked on my college project and played some video games. How was your evening? You were not home last night. You work really hard for cases."

Kiara smiled, appreciating Brent's concern. "Thank you, Brent, my love. Your words mean a lot to me. I promise to take care of myself."

"Alright, let's just get ready for family dinner. Do you remember that, right, honey? Erica and Jason might be waiting for us. We need to be together."

Brent, brimming with enthusiasm, "Oh, yes! See you in the evening, Mom."

Kiara nodded in agreement and went to her room. The intriguing moments of the previous night lingered in her mind again. Excusing herself for a moment, she checked her phone, hoping to find a message or a sign of Mr. Romano's presence. But in vain.

The evening sun cast a warm glow as they got ready for dinner, their faces adorned with smiles and anticipation. The table was set with care, the aroma of a home-cooked meal wafting through the air.

Kiara, a devoted mother with two sons, Jason and Brent, cherished the moments she spent with them and her daughter-in-law.

She felt happy! Everything felt happy around her!

No matter what happens, nothing can set us apart. Kiara thought.

Chapter 4
High Stakes

•••

It's going to be a lovely weekend, that's what people think of it. Beautiful sunshine, cloudless skies, and a cool breeze, but there was nothing.

In the old days, we might have driven to Greenwood Vale with a picnic and spent all afternoon lying on a blanket in dappled sunlight, playing with kids and drinking wine. We might have barbecued with our old friends or gone to Miami for a beach party.

Living like this, the way Carol had been living at the moment, makes everything much harder. There's so much darkness, exhaustion, and sadness. She closed her eyes and let the darkness grow into something worse: a memory, a flashback.

I must come to terms with it; resisting won't change a thing. The impending doom will linger throughout life, undulating in waves—intense, then subdued, only to resurge with a relentless grip. That twisting sensation in the pit of her stomach began with the pangs of shame. The heat flushed on her face, and the involuntary squeeze of her eyes as if willing it all to vanish.

She was sitting on the terrace, waiting for the rain. The sky is black above her, swallows looping and diving, the air thick with moisture.

Dan will be home in an hour or so, and I'll have to tell him. The only person who'll be disappointed is Dan, so I have to think of something to tell him. He'll only be pissed off for a minute or two, and I'll make it up to him. And I won't just be sitting around the house all day. I have been making plans for a long time so I can take a photography course and have my blogging page or learn to cook.

I quit! Yes, I quit!

She felt so much better as if anything was possible.

I'm free! She exclaimed to herself.

The next morning, Carol awoke with the early light, having a few hours of sleep this time — a marked improvement from her previous week. Emerging from bed, she felt refreshment, a rare sensation that prompted her to forgo her usual spot on the terrace, but this time, she opted for a brisk walk instead.

As Carol peacefully slept through the quiet night, a sudden disturbance jolted her awake. The eerie sound of screeching, persistent and haunting, pierced the stillness around her.

Someone was crying and yelling!

She got up in the night, left Dan sleeping, and sneaked down to the rooftop. With trepidation gnawing at her, she climbed the stairs.

The dim glow of the hallway barely illuminated her path as she reached the top landing.

Just as she reached for the doorknob, an inexplicable force seized her, Stop! Wrenching her backward with a violent ferocity. DO NOT GO!

Carol spoke out into the darkness, "Hello, is anyone here? Just let go of me?" she yelled.

Carol stood beneath the starry night sky and looked up at the constellation. Unpredictably, a shadowy figure stepped out from behind.

This mysterious assailant struck Carol on the nape of her neck in an abrupt and unanticipated assault as Carol struggled but fell off the ground.

In a sudden surge of fear and desperation, Carol's voice pierced the stillness of the night as she let out a loud and urgent cry for help.

"HELP! HELP"

"DAN, DAN, PLEASE, I NEED HELP!"

"HELP!"

Dan swiftly approached, and he found Carol alone lying on the floor – there was no one else, just Carol, her head stained with blood dripping down her face.

Dan rushed to Carol's side, his eyes widening in disbelief at seeing her injured. "Oh my God, Carol, what happened?" he exclaimed.

In the grip of searing pain, Carol fought to regain her composure, her face contorted with discomfort. "I don't know, Dan," she stammered, her voice laden with unease. "I heard this... sssss... some noise, and then, someone— someone attacked me from behind."

Upon waking up the next morning, Carol felt a bandage tightly wrapped around her head.

Dan was sitting in front of her, and nobody said anything; he just looked at her expectantly. "What's going on, Carol?" he inquired gently.

She hesitated in her initial response, a reflexive defense. "Nothing," she replied.

"Just look at yourself; what's going on here? Why do you keep hearing these strange voices at night?"

"Dan, I don't know why this is happening."

He looked into her eyes, trying to make sense of the unsettling things she had been going through.

"That's not entirely true. Something is bothering you. I can sense it. There are things you hear at home. That screeching sound in the backyard, and now, with what happened last night, someone attacked you, and there was no one on the terrace."

"Dan, it's just been... overwhelming. I can't shake this feeling like something is not right. Last night was just the breaking point for me. I felt attacked, and there was no one there. I don't know how to make sense of it." Carol said, sobbing.

"I don't know who or what I'm dealing with, but I can't ignore it anymore. I need to find out the truth. Maybe it's time for you to consider seeking professional help, Carol. Therapy will help you."

"I'm not insane, Dan." Carol clarified.

"It's not about being insane, Carol. A therapist can

provide guidance, help you untangle your thoughts, and offer tools to cope. You don't have to carry the burden by yourself."

"Dan, please," Carol pleaded, her voice strained with emotion as tears streamed down her cheeks.

"If you can't share whatever is going on with me, I might suggest you go for therapy." Dan sighed, realizing the depth of Carol's distress.

"It's not that I don't want to share with you. It's just... it's really complicated. I'm dealing with some personal struggles, and I don't want to burden you with them."

"But keeping things secret from each other will only make it harder for both of us," Dan responded.

"Yeah, I think I should consider therapy, Dan. It's just hard to open up about certain things."

"I'm here for you, Carol, but at least give it a try. For both of us and our children."

Carol took a nap in the afternoon. When she woke up, Dan left for work, and she felt worried and guilty. She felt guilty, just not too much. But these days, she had been badly stuck. Couldn't focus on her husband, children, and cases.

Carol thought about Dan leaving for work and telling

her about the therapy sessions. She just had hazy memories of what happened.

He was dressed, looking at her concerned. It wasn't exactly anger or contempt—it was a request. A humble request.

It's ridiculous when I think about it. How did I find myself here? I wonder where it started, my decline; I wonder at what point I could have halted it. Where did I take the wrong turn? Carol thought.

She felt nervous and started walking around the house, but couldn't relax. It's like someone was here while she was sleeping. Everything looked normal, but the house felt strange, like things were touched or moved a bit. As she walked, it seemed like someone else was here, always just out of her sight. She checked the doors to the garden three times, but they were locked.

Upon returning to her living room, Carol noticed a piece of paper on the table.

She was rendered motionless by an overwhelming wave of terror. **IT WAS BLOOD!**

I can't live here, and I simply can't.

She really wanted Dan to come home. She needed him. Panic intensified, fueled by the eerie circumstances surrounding her. Carol clutched her phone and dialed Dan's number. There's a silence, and tears welled up in her eyes when Dan didn't pick up her calls.

Carol texted him:

> Give me a ring, OK? And come straight home.

•••

Kiara's phone beeps. There's a message on it, received hours ago. It's Carol.

I don't want to hear what she has to say, but I have to, I can't ignore her.

She opened the text:

> I've to tell you something. Can we meet at Coffee Uptown Café? Around 3:00 p.m.

Kiara gave her phone a look and replied, "Okay, sure."

Once reached, Kiara noticed a major difference in Carol's demeanor when they both reached the designated location. Carol appeared noticeably paler than her normally lively self. She had a bandage on her head.

As they sat in the Coffee Uptown Café, Kiara couldn't contain her curiosity any longer. Leaning forward, she asked Carol the reason for the meetup. "Did Dan do something to you?"

Carol remained silent. She held her hand up and gulped water.

"Why are you in this awful condition? Did your husband do this to you?" Kiara taunted her again. "You haven't worked in days, right? Or weeks? Do you know how idiotic I felt? What an idiot Dan feels."

"Kiara…."

"Honestly, Carol. Please, please tell me that you have another job that you just haven't told me about or Dan. Please tell me that you haven't been pretending to go to work. You have been lying to me—day in, day out—all this time."

"I didn't know how to tell you…"

"You didn't know how to tell me? How about: 'Carol is getting insane."

"I'm sorry, but honestly, Kiara. I'm not insane. I was here to tell you something."

She just said, "Oh, that's a shame; you have to tell me something."

I could tell she didn't mean it. She's angry.

Carol realized she could no longer bear the burden of her fears when they met. Accidents, nightmares, and endless fatigue weighed heavily on her heart.

Kiara could see her expression at that distance and realized that she had felt alone for a very long time. Carol is kind and soft, everything that a woman should be. Kiara contemplated. While Kiara had been a strong and protective woman, she could make intellectual leaps and dissect and analyze problems.

Kiara was upset with Carol. She didn't tell her about the case hearing, and Kiara felt let down because she thought they were good friends. Kiara also reminded Carol that she was her boss and expected better.

Summoning great courage, Carol decided to confide in Kiara about the unsettling case that had been haunting her.

"I've been warned," Carol admitted, her voice steady but laced with anxiety. "Someone unknown has been pressuring me to release certain details related to the case. I didn't know where else to turn, Kiara, so I needed to tell you."

Kiara, however, remained skeptical. "Carol, you are lying to me again," she responded, her tone edged with doubt. "You are a soft-hearted person, and this seems like an excuse to release that criminal because you didn't want to punish him. What's the real story here? You have avoided me for weeks, and now you have come to justify yourself with a bunch of craps."

Carol, feeling the weight of Kiara's accusations, took a deep breath before explaining herself. "Kiara, I understand how it may seem, but I did nothing to compromise the case. My family's life is at risk, and I've been receiving threats from that UNC caller. They warned me about the consequences if I didn't cooperate. I had to tell you; I'm scared for my family."

Kiara's expression softened slightly, but doubt still lingered in her eyes. "Carol, threats or not, compromising the case puts everyone at risk."

Tears welled up in Carol's eyes as she continued, her voice trembling with fear and desperation. "Kiara, someone has been looking out for me, and I've been followed at home. They've even given me threats, telling me that I shall die soon." Carol unfolded the paper, the one with the ominous message written in blood, and showed it to Kiara.

Kiara's expression shifted from skepticism to genuine concern as she observed the distress etched on Carol's face.

"WHAT!!!! You are telling me now, Judge Carol Hidding?" she exclaimed.

Carol nodded, tears welling up in her eyes. "I didn't know who to turn to, Kiara. I thought you needed to know, especially if it's connected to the case. I've been scared for my family, and I didn't want to put them in more danger."

Kiara's initial skepticism gave way to a genuine worry. "Carol, I had no idea you were going through this. We need to get you to help and ensure your safety. But we must also find a way to handle these threats without compromising the case. Let's work together on this. But I need the whole truth from you. No more half-truths or excuses. Can you do that?"

Carol nodded in agreement, and Kiara hugged her.

Exiting the cafe, Carol led Kiara to her office. Carol's hands shook slightly as she reached for the file.

"Provide me with all the files, Carol. Arrest Warrants,

Affidavits, statements, search warrants, court orders, everything. I'll kill this bastard."

Carol opened the files and laid them out for Kiara to see. The revelation was swift as Kiara's eyes fell upon the name written in bold letters: Salvatore Romano.

"Salvatore Romano? Carol, is this the person who was released?" she asked.

It might be someone else. Kiara prayed. I know he isn't something else.

Carol nodded solemnly, her eyes avoiding Kiara's gaze momentarily. "Yes, Kiara. Salvatore Romano was released. He's the man connected to the threats and the warnings. According to the detectives working on the case, they found him from the Coastal Suite."
"The Coastal Suite, you sure?" Kiara asked.

"Yes, everything is in front of you, Kiara. What else do you need?"

Kiara's mind raced to process this unexpected twist. "Salvatore Romano... I didn't know."

As Kiara continued to sift through the case files, a sudden memory flashed through Kiara's mind.

A few days ago, I was in Mr. Romano's room, and I noticed the initials 'SR' on one of his shirts. The one was hanging in his bathroom. It makes sense now. Kiara's mind was full of questions, and she needed answers. She loves a man who is a member of a drug cartel.

Driven by a sense of urgency, Kiara swiftly left Carol's office and made her way to the Coastal Suite. The tires of her car screeched against the pavement as she navigated the city streets.

I need to look into this Coastal Suite and find out more about his whereabouts.

Upon arriving at the Coastal Suite, Kiara hurriedly approached the entrance, her eyes scanning the surroundings. However, the suite seemed quiet, and there was no sign of Salvatore Romano. The realization that he wasn't there intensified the gravity of the situation.

Where could he be? She muttered to herself, her mind racing through the possibilities. *I'LL KILL HIM.*

Kiara took a deep breath, contemplating her next move.

It's worse, so much worse than I imagined.

Velvet Olive Restaurant..... Yes, got it!

The realization struck Kiara like a bolt of lightning. She vividly recalled the day they first met—Mr. Romano had followed her to the parking lot and then disappeared into the nearby Larch woods. The pieces of the puzzle started to fit together in her mind.

Perhaps he had been living somewhere near those woods. I will put that rascal behind the bars.

Kiara wasted no time. Fueled by this revelation, she rushed back to her car and headed toward the location where she had encountered Mr. Romano.

The parking lot was bustling with people, Kiara stood there and looked at everyone. There was no trace of him.

Kiara walked into the woods with a gun in her hand. The memory of Romano vanishing into the woods on that previous encounter replayed in her mind, urging her to stay vigilant.

Where the fuck are you? I'll shoot you.

The woods enveloped Kiara as she approached the mysterious cabin in the center of the dense forest.

Just as her hand grazed the handle, a voice came from behind.

"Don't!!! DON'T YOU DARE!!! "Are you looking out for me?"

Kiara froze, the hairs on the back of her neck standing on end. Slowly turning around, she found herself face to face with Mr. Romano, who had emerged from the shadows of tall trees.

He knew that I was looking out for him. Damn! Damn it! He's a bastard.

It's darker still and getting cold.

I'm sure of it, but I look up, and Romano is there, his eyes on mine, his expression soft. He's listening. He wants me to tell him something. My mouth becomes dry. It felt so strange to be with him.

"Hello, Mr. Salvatore Romano. How have you been? Do you like being released from the jail?"

"Say my name again. I want you to say my name over and over again."

"Well, fuck off. Does that even make sense?" Kiara replied angrily. "The story about your family was a lie, and you twisted it all around. You lied all the time about everything. Even when you didn't need to, even when there was no point. You are a drug dealer, right? I really want to shoot you here right now."

Romano's eyes locked onto Kiara's, a hint of challenge in his gaze. "So, you know everything now?" he inquired, a subtle smirk playing on his lips.

Kiara, unyielding in her determination, met his gaze squarely. "Yes, I know. I want you to spend the rest of your life in jail," she asserted firmly.

"Why do you care so much, Kiara? We had something, remember? I love you and can't resist staying away from you. I know you love me too."

Kiara's eyes hardened, the memories of their past encounters flooding back. "What we had is irrelevant now. You're a criminal, and you've threatened someone I care about. That changes everything."

"One day, we had love-making, and this day, we are fighting." Mr. Romano defended.

"I don't care about your excuses, Romano, or should I call you Mr. Salvatore Romano? The law will decide your fate," Kiara retorted, her hand tightening around the grip of her gun.

"That was a task and a purpose that I had been given, Kiara. You need to understand this."

"A task? What are you talking about, Romano? What purpose? You are a criminal, and you are supposed to be in jail."

"I may be a bad man for you, but I love you. Since the day I saw you in the court, I always wanted you and wanted to spend the rest of my life with you, Kiara."

"Love? Romano, you've threatened and terrorized

someone. Love doesn't justify criminal actions. There's a line you've crossed."

"Kiara, there's more to this than you know. The people I'm involved with, they're dangerous. They had me do things, and I thought if I followed their orders, I could have a chance at a different life, a life with you."
Kiara struggled to process the conflicting emotions. "You think your actions are justified because you claim to love me? Romano, you're responsible for your choices. I will put you in jail and the people you are working for. I will go deeper to catch all the criminals."

"It's really dangerous, Kiara. Politicians and high-profile people are involved. They are really powerful people who won't hesitate to protect their interests. If you go after them, you'll be putting your life on the line. It's a life-and-death game."

"I don't care. If there are criminals involved, they will face justice."

"Kiara, you don't understand. It's not that simple. If you do something, if you push too hard, you'll be killed."

"I understand more than you think," she retorted with determination. She continued. "I'll catch them, not here but in front of a lot of people. He will beg me for his life, and I'll shoot them."

"You can't, Kiara, because you love me."

"Huh!!! Run for your life." She replied and left the place.

The next day, the number that threatened Carol had been tracked down, according to Kiara's informants, who had disclosed a breakthrough. It led to someone who made the call from a yacht.

THAT WAS MR. ROMANO'S FAMILY YACHT.

As the evening broke, the harbor came ablaze with action by the cops as they geared themselves to raid the yacht they suspected of being the hub of the illicit operations.

The police, armed and determined, stormed the yacht. As Kiara and her team stormed the yacht, a vortex of violence engulfed them. Buildings erupted in flames, cars became collateral damage, and the yacht's pristine decks were tainted with the blood of those involved in the drug-selling operation. Amidst the chaos, the police apprehended Damien, a high-ranking member of the Drug Cartel Mafia, surrounded by tons of illicit substances. But it wasn't Damien who had threatened

Carol's life, but someone far more elusive and cunning.

The night, still heavy with the aftermath of the yacht raid, Kiara went again to the mysterious woods.

Kiara approached the door and knocked. The door opened. It was Mr. Romano on the other side; they kissed passionately, and she went inside.

THE NEXT MORNING

•••

It was a BIG day. The President of the United States nominated Judge Kiara to the highest Court in America. She was bestowed a prestigious honor for her unparalleled bravery and courage against the insidious grip of crime head-on.

Judge Kiara garnered praise from the media for her dedication to promoting justice and equality. However, neither the Supreme Court nor the President were aware of Judge Kiara's involvement with Mr. Romano, a member of the drug cartel and an illegal arms dealer.

After receiving accolades from the US President, Kiara returned to her office, where Jessica awaited her arrival.

"Congratulations! You truly deserve this recognition, Kiara." Jessica praised warmly.

"Thank you, Jessica. Your support means the world to me," Kiara replied with gratitude, her voice tinged with appreciation.

Chapter 5
Hollow Victory

Brent's college life was different from many others. He didn't stay with his mom or dad; instead, he had a place on the college campus all to himself. But he wasn't really alone because he had a cool friend named Jay. They were more than just friends; they were best friends, living in the same building.

Brent and Jay did a lot of things together. They studied late into the night, went on fun adventures, and shared a lot of laughs.

Brent was up before dawn, startled awake by a dream. It was unusual for him. Today was the big day for Brent – the basketball tournament match. As he opened his eyes, he quickly got out of bed and started getting ready. He knew that being prepared was key for the game ahead.

Brent put on his basketball jersey and shorts, lacing

up his sneakers tightly. With each tug of the laces, he felt the anticipation building. He checked his bag, making sure he had everything he needed – a water bottle, towel, and, of course, his lucky basketball. With everything ready, Brent headed towards the court.

Within an hour, Kiara dressed swiftly, settled into her Range Rover, and headed to the basketball court.

Upon arrival, she spotted her ex-husband and his pregnant wife. With a sigh, Kiara muttered to herself, Ugh, why are they here? I hate seeing them both.

Mr. John Madders, Kiara's ex-husband, is the top detective in Miami, and he is loved and respected by everyone in the town. Mr. Madders chose a different path in life, and he left Kiara for a younger woman.

Once they reached the basketball court, Judge Kiara Tierson found herself in a situation where she had to see Mr. Madders and his wife, Diane. But Kiara chose not to talk to them. She was there for her son Brent, not for these people.

Kiara headed straight to the stands, quickly finding a good seat. Meanwhile, Mr. Madders and his wife were seated on the opposite side, and Kiara ensured to avoid interaction with them.

The scoreboard displayed the team names:

"Thunder Hawks" vs. "Ravens."

Brent was a Thunder Hawk. Kiara felt a surge of pride and joy for him. She was happy for her youngest son.

Brent, who's really good at basketball, was again playing like a pro. He dribbled the ball super smoothly and moved past the other players like a ninja. His throw to the hoop was perfect as he crossed the floor's tall line, and the ball went in! Applause and chants erupted from the audience. Despite the other team's best efforts, Brent's Thunder Hawks squad ultimately prevailed. They scored points by passing the ball to one another and doing awesome moves. They won!

Thunder Hawks were super happy, giving high-fives and hugs. Brent looked up to the stands, and there were Kiara and John, his mom and dad, smiling and cheering for him. They were so proud!

Kiara, shouting over the cheers: "Love you, Brent, my baby! You played amazing out there! I'm proud of you."

Brent, still catching his breath but grinning ear to ear, mouthed a "thank you" to his mom in the stands.

Brent became a shining star. Basketball fans and scouts were captivated by his outstanding abilities on the court after another victory.

Once out of the court, Brent came to Kiara and hugged her tightly. "I did it, Mom." He said excitedly. They both cheered and laughed.

A voice emanated from behind; it was John Madders saying, "Hey Brent, well played. We enjoyed the game."

Diane also complimented Brent, saying, "You performed excellently, Brent."

He responded with gratitude, "Thank you, Dad and Diane, and thanks for being here."

Kiara remained silent in response to John Madders and Diane; she chose not to say anything.

Meanwhile, Kiara's phone chimed with a message from Carol. She glanced at the screen:

Damien is killed!

Coming in a while.

"Is everything okay, Mom?" Brent asked.

"Oh, that's nothing, honey. Just got an update about a case that I'm working on." Kiara reassured smilingly.

"So, when are we doing to have a party to celebrate Brent's victory?" she continued.

"Whenever you say, Mom."

"Really? So, let's plan a family dinner for tomorrow with Jason and Erica. I've got a surprise for you." Kiara's eyes sparkled with a mischievous glint as she hinted at the forthcoming celebration.

"Okay, done, Mom," Brent responded happily.

"Honey, now, I need to head home to pick up some files; there's an urgent case I must handle."

As Brent and Kiara were engrossed in conversation, Mr. Madders and Diane bid their goodbyes and left the premises.

Kiara asked Brent, "Honey, if you want, you can come home. I can talk to your school teacher, and we can have fun together."

Brent realized that he had some important work to do, "Actually, Mom, I've got some work to finish. So, I'll stay here."

"What work, honey? Why don't you just come home for a few hours with me?"

Brent explained, "Umm…. Mom, I want to celebrate my victory with some friends. You know Jay will be waiting for me. But I'll join you at dinner."

"Alright, honey. I will text you the place and time. Enjoy yourself."

Brent, giving a reassuring smile, nodded, "Will do, Mom."

"Take care, baby. We'll continue the celebration when I'm back from work.

Brent nodded with a smile, "Sure, Mom. See you later."

She hugged him tightly for a minute, and then she got into the car.

Brent approached Jay with a smile on his face. "Jay, my man! We did it!" Brent exclaimed. "The college is throwing us a party tonight to celebrate. You in?"

Jay, masking the turbulence of his inner thoughts with a forced smile, nodded in agreement. "Sure, Brent. Let's celebrate."

As they made their way to the celebratory venue in college, the air buzzed with the shared joy of success.

"Can you believe it? I'm on my way to the NBA! That's a huge thing, and I'll live my dreams." Brent told him.

Jay forced a smile, trying to hide the subtle pang of

envy that prickled within him.

"What!!! I mean, yeah, Brent, it's amazing. Congrats, buddy." Jay nodded, but his mind was racing with conflicting emotions.

Once reached, Brent was surrounded by his well-wishers. His teammates, teachers, and coaches showered him with congratulations, their faces beaming with pride.

Coach Thompson, a seasoned mentor, clapped Brent on the back with genuine warmth. "Brent, you have made us all proud. This is your ticket to the NBA, my boy. You've worked hard for it."

"You're destined for greatness, Brent. The NBA awaits, and you have earned every bit of it." Mr. Matthews, Brent's other teacher, said.

As Jay stood on the periphery of the celebration, he wasn't feeling good at all. Jay felt really sad as he stayed on the edge of the happy party. He just wanted to be by himself in his room. The people having fun made him even more unhappy. It felt like everyone was having a good time except him. All the noise and laughter made him want to be alone.

When he finally got to his room, he closed the door behind him. The room was quiet and a bit dark. It felt like a different world from the lively party happening outside. Jay sat alone, trying to understand why he felt so down. The night that was supposed to be fun turned into a lonely time for him.

JUDGE KIARA'S OFFICE

●●●

The message about Damien's death had left Kiara with a sense of urgency. Once settled into her chair, she immediately dialed Carol's number, asking her to come to her office.

"Damien was killed in the jail. The circumstances are unclear. Nobody has seen or heard anything. We're still piecing together the information, but he killed."

"But how does something like this happen without anyone noticing? What about the time it happened? Wasn't there anyone around? Any CCTV footage?"

"The incident occurred around 3 in the morning when the jail remains relatively quiet. Unfortunately, there wasn't any CCTV footage in that area."

"How could this be possible, Carol? Someone should have heard something."

"I agree, Kiara. The police and detectives are

pulling all the strings to uncover the truth. But there's more – Damien's body has been sent for an autopsy."

"Autopsy? That's great. What did they find?"

"The autopsy findings are expected later in the evening. Currently, the cause of the incident and the responsible party remain unknown. It looks like someone deliberately administered something harmful."

"Someone targeted Damien. I'm considering the possibility that he might have had important information related to the drug cartel."

"There are chances." Carol nodded in agreement.

"Anything else, Kiara," Carol asked.

"Ah, no, thank you, Carol," Kiara replied.

As Carol prepared to leave her office, Kiara asked, "How are you holding up, Carol?" She went right to the point, as she always does.

"It's been difficult, but I'm okay. Thanks for help."

In response, Kiara offered support, saying, "If you need anything, anything at all, I'm here for you."

After Carol was gone, Kiara received a message from her boss, Jessica Reynolds.

Meet me in my office right now.

"Hey, Jessica. What's up?"

"Hi, Kiara, how's everything going? I have been thinking about you."

"Really? What do you need me to do?"

"I want you to lead the investigation into Damien's death. You've shown great skills in handling tough cases before, and considering you were the one who found him on the yacht, I trust you to dig into this."

"I appreciate the trust, Jessica. But…."

"This is a good offer for a woman in your position to consider. Since you are already outside the multijurisdictional mess and, therefore, immune to it, why don't you keep it that way? Work with the Federal Bureau?" Jessica continued. "I can give you access to all the information we get as soon as we get it. I will give you everything you need in terms of resources and information and all of our current data."

I need to find out the unknown UNC caller, too. He would try to create a mess again. It will be going to happen soon. Kiara thought.

"Kiara, you are the best person who can do her job exceptionally. I can trust no one else. You agree with me, right, Kiara?"

"Agree, Jessica," Kiara said.

"Great!" Jessica responded. "To ensure you have the support you need for Damien's case, I've assigned Agent Ethan Steele to work with you. I believe you both make a good team."

"Agent Steele? That's great news, Jessica."

"Start working on it, and please keep me updated regularly. It's a big case, and we need to ensure that everything goes well. People are eagerly seeking answers, and the media is stirring up attention."

"I will, Jessica."

Jessica and Kiara talked some more about his offer, and she was able to pin her down on a few specifics.

Basically, she was sold, though. Working with Jessica would give her access to a first-rate support team, and she has clout whenever she needs it. She wouldn't be alone anymore.

They ordered burgers and more wine and continued to talk and put the final touches on her deal with the Devil. For the first time, she was feeling a little hopeful while working with Jessica.

By the time Kiara got back to her office, it was very late. She got a bunch of texts from Jason and Brent.

I'm here.

Where are you, Mom?

We are at Pier's Grill House, waiting for you.

Kiara called Jason, anyway. She always calls him when she's away, twice every day, morning and night.

"Hey, Jason, I'm stuck with a case. It's urgent. Can you handle everything there? I will make up to Brent afterward."

Jason inquired, "Is it truly urgent? We're all waiting for you here – Brent and Erica."

Kiara sighed, "Jason, I wish I could be there with all of you, but this case needs my immediate attention."

Jason, understanding the nature of his mom's work, nodded and said, "Alright, Mom. Relax yourself. I'll handle it here. Brent will understand, too. We'll catch up soon."

"Thanks, Jason. I really appreciate your support. I will try to wrap this up quickly."

After she hung up the call with Jason, Kiara started thinking about the case. Several instances were still active nationwide during that week. Each one of them included hundreds of pages of in-depth FBI briefs that she read.

Texan who murders homosexual males in Austin. A serial murderer in Michigan's Ann Arbor and

Kalamazoo areas who targets elderly men. Chicago, North Palm Beach, Long Island, Oakland, and Berkeley include drug dealers who are pattern killers, too.

Her eyes ached from reading, and she felt much worse on the inside. The killer was winning so far. He seemed invincible and uncatchable. He didn't make any mistakes and didn't leave any clues. He was very sure of himself…

Anger and violation fused in her mind. Adrenaline surged powerfully through her body. Kiara, determined to get answers about Damien's death, opted to meet Romano in person. She hopped into her car and headed towards his location. Before her arrival, she dropped a message, I'll be there around 11."

She received no response from Romano.

Once reached, she saw the black Ford parked in Romano's wood driveway. He's inside. Kiara heard him mutter something unintelligible in a low, harsh voice on the phone. "This is crossing the line now. Give me a little space on this one. I will call you back." Romano said sternly before disconnecting the call.

Kiara wondered what was bothering him so much. She went inside, and they kissed. Kiara pulled back and asked him about the call. "What happened? You seemed upset on the phone. Is everything okay?"

Mr. Romano took a deep breath, his eyes reflecting frustration.

"It was Diego Ramos asking me to come and meet him. He thinks that I'm working for the police. He's an asshole. I needed to get it out of my system. Trust me, I'm."

"What does Diego Ramos want? And why does he think you're working for the police?" Kiara interrogated curiously.

"Kiara, it's because he saw you with me, and you're a judge," he explained. "His men have been keeping an eye on me, and unfortunately, they know about you too. So, when Damien was caught by you, people started investigating his boss, Ramos, too. The authorities intensified their focus on Ramos after Damien's capture."

"But someone killed that guy in the jail, and I assume you know everything," Kiara asked.

"I know nothing, Kiara."

"I heard you talking on the call. What was that? I would love to hear that the killer might be Ramos."

There was silence… blessed silence…. Nobody

spoke anything.

"No, Ramos cannot kill Damien. He can never do this." Curious, Kiara inquired, "Why not?"

Mr. Romano grudgingly said, "Because Damien was his son, Kiara," breaking the awkward moment.

"Then who killed Damien inside the jail? I want to know, Salvatore. Ramos isn't that person. Then who is responsible?"

"I wish I had all the answers, Kiara. But right now, I'm just as puzzled as you are."

"You aren't listening to me, Romano. A drug smuggler has been brutally murdered inside the jail. I caught this man from your yacht with his men three days ago. The police will somehow consider me linked with the case, which I'm not. Carol was getting calls from someone. She's afraid as hell. I need to protect her. She's not safe. We're standing on the edge of something dangerous, and we need to act fast to unravel the truth before it consumes all of us."

"Kiara. I'm willing to listen, but I must tell you, I know nothing about Damien's death. The people I deal with are dangerous. They can kill anyone, anywhere!"

Kiara turned furious; she took a pause and said, "I

understand the gravity of the situation. But staying silent won't make us safer. I need to expose the truth to ensure justice is served. I appreciate your honesty when you shared about Diego Ramos, but it's not enough. I need to know everything about the drug cartel and their illicit activities. Damien's life was taken, and we need to bring those responsible to justice."

"Kiara, I've already told you as much as I can."

"If you don't disclose everything, I will have no choice but to involve myself in this case."

"Kiara, you don't know what you're getting into. These people are dangerous."

"I need to act; otherwise, they will continue to harm lives. I need to save Carol's life, Romano."

Kiara left the cabin and walked towards her car. She was angry.

As she approached the car, Mr. Romano spoke from behind, "I can't lose you, Kiara."

He came, took her hand, looked into her eyes, and said, "Kiara, I love you too much to see you in harm's way. The mayor, Jonathan Strohm, is deeply connected with the drug cartel. It's not just about me; it's about the safety of everyone I care about. It's about you. We will face this together."

"Loving you doesn't mean that I will leave those BASTARDS!!!"

"I know, Kiara and I will help you out. We both will find out."

They had an adorable moment together under a moonlit sky. They sealed their commitment in the middle of uncertainty with a passionate kiss. They assured each other that they would stand with one another through thick and thin, and they exchanged quiet messages of love and unity.

When Kiara got home, it was super late, like 6 am. The house was all quiet, and everyone was about to wake up. Kiara went to her room, took a shower, and went to the kitchen. Jason and Erica were at the breakfast table, and Kiara shared the news about Mr. Romano with them. They couldn't have been happier.

With a big smile, she told them that very soon, she and Mr. Romano would be getting engaged. She also let them know that he would soon be joining them to live together as a family.

In the meantime, Kiara's phone rang, and the caller ID displayed Carol's name. With a silent sigh, Kiara answered the call.

"Hey, Carol, all good," she said.

"Kiara, I just got some new information about Damien's case. I have emailed you a few documents. Please check."

"Okay, sure. Thanks, Carol."

THE NEXT DAY

●●●

Following endless administrative meetings at the highest levels, Kiara left with Agent Ethan Steele to Damien's residence. She told him everything that had happened so far.

He would be coming after someone else now. It might be Carol. He had to try to catch her, and he'd kill her if he did. Although Kiara had horrible thoughts, she was strong enough to ignore them.

It appeared like any other apartment when Kiara and Ethan arrived at Damien's place.

As they moved through the apartment, Kiara and Agent Steele looked for any signs that could help them understand what led to Damien's tragic end.

The kitchen was stocked with culinary gadgetry,

and fine wines were chilling in the fridge. The living room has some lovely crystals on display in the cabinets, but there are no pictures or anything else that could give us clues about his personal life. The apartment had three bedrooms. The smallest and the biggest one.

"I will look here," Kiara said. "I'll take the bedrooms," Ethan said.

Before she could say more to Ethan, something crashed deep inside the apartment, and they heard someone running. Kiara drew her weapon and hissed, "Ethan, around the back." Ethan pivoted and ran, looking for a way into the alley. At the same time, Kiara went through Damien's place with the gun up and moving quickly. She took notes of a few possessions.

"Without a doubt, he was an athlete and a powerful runner. Despite toting a black knapsack, he continued to leap rather than run, gaining distance from me as he devoured the ground." Ethan came back and informed Kiara.

"I found a laptop still open. Seems someone who was in this place might have taken something from it. Something really important."

Recognizing the potential significance of the open

laptop, they carefully secured it in an evidence bag.

There was a lot to absorb. It's all messed up! Damien sat between the cold prison cells, and someone killed him.

In Kiara's office, Kiara and Ethan talked about Damien's autopsy report. They looked at the papers that had information about how Damien died.

An overdose of a chemical was determined to be the cause of death for Damien in the autopsy report. It didn't seem like a natural death, and the report's findings raised suspicions about what might have happened.

Kiara finally turned around. Curiosity and terror got the best of her.

"Apparently, when Damien woke up, he might have immediately known that something was very wrong and something would get worse. His vision got blurred. His pulse turned jumpy. He might have gone from extreme feelings of detachment to depression to panic in just a few moments he had been conscious. Maybe the killer had given him Klonopin, Kiara considered. It is an antianxiety medication. However, he would likely face similar adverse effects if the killer started him on a high dosage, maybe five to 10 milligrams. Alternatively, perhaps he had taken Marinol pills? For nausea that might occur as a side effect of chemotherapy, they were prescribed. He would be maniacal if he gave him, say, 200 mg daily. Cottonmouth is a type of frog, it's freaking insane. Depression with manic episodes. A deadly dosage would range from 1,500 to 2,000 mg. He couldn't fight him like this."

Astonished by Kiara's expertise, Agent Ethan was amazed.

Kiara looked into Damien's past appearance to try to remember him before the black eyes. The face had unsightly swelling under the eyes and the jaw.

The meeting was halted when Jason, Kiara's oldest son, called her, asking if everything was okay. He had heard the news about Damien's death on the news, and concern filled his voice as he sought reassurance about the safety of his mother.

Erica and Jason were married and expecting a child. Jason is a busy man, always working hard to make their lives better, but he knows how to take care of his family.

"Hey, Mom, how's everything? You didn't come to the dinner, and Dad told us that something important came up."

"Everything is okay on my end, Jason. It's a tough situation, but we're working on it. It's just a case. How are you and Erica holding up?"

"We're are good, Mom. Erica and I just got worried about you."

"Right now, we're focusing on the investigation. Thanks for checking in, sweetheart."

The next day, Kiara gathered her family together at home. With a nervous but excited smile, she shared some big news. "I want to tell you all something important," she began, her voice filled with emotion. "I'm in love with a man named Mr. Romano, and we've decided to get engaged."

Jason and Erica's eyes widened in surprise, but soon, smiles spread across their faces as they realized the depth of Kiara's happiness. They gathered around her, offering hugs and congratulations, their hearts filled with joy for her newfound love.

"Oh, Mom, that's wonderful!" Erica exclaimed, her eyes sparkling with joy. "We can't wait to meet him," Jason said.

"Can we meet him?" Jason asked.

"Of course, sweetheart. He's actually in his car outside of our house. I asked him to come over. I will call him in. I know you'll like him." Kiara said.

"What!!! Bring him inside, Mom." Erica said.

"Yes, please bring him in," Jason added eagerly.

As Kiara stepped outside to invite Mr. Romano into the house, Jason and Erica exchanged excited glances, their anticipation growing with each passing moment. They couldn't wait to meet the man who had captured their daughter's heart and brought such happiness into her life.

As Mr. Romano entered the house, he greeted Jason and Erica with a warm smile. "Hello, Jason and Erica. It's a pleasure to meet you both," he said, extending his hand in a friendly gesture.

Jason shook his hand firmly, a welcoming grin spreading across his face. "Likewise, Mr. Romano," he replied. "We're glad to finally meet you."

Erica nodded in agreement, her eyes shining with warmth. "Yes, we have heard so much about you," she said, her voice filled with genuine interest. "We're excited to get to know you better."

Mr. Romano returned their smiles, feeling grateful

for their warm welcome. "Thank you for having me," he said sincerely. "I care deeply for Kiara, and I'm honored to be here with all of you today."

As everyone settled into conversation, they shared their excitement about their upcoming engagement.

"Jason, Erica," Kiara began with a radiant smile, "I have something exciting to share with you both. Mr. Romano and I have decided to get engaged, and we're planning to do it this Saturday."

Jason and Erica exchanged delighted glances, their faces lighting up with happiness. "Really! That's such a

"Mr. Romano is a lucky man to have you," Jason said, and everyone smiled.

"I've been thinking a lot about how we should celebrate our engagement," Mr. Romano said, his eyes lighting up with enthusiasm. "And I have an idea that I think you'll love."

"What is it?" Kiara asked.

"I thought it would be magical to have our engagement on my luxurious yacht," Mr. Romano revealed, a smile playing at the corners of his lips. "We could have a beautiful ceremony surrounded by the sea and the stars."

Judge Kiara's eyes widened in delight. "That sounds absolutely perfect," she exclaimed, her heart fluttering with excitement. "I can't think of a more romantic setting."

They continued to discuss the details of their engagement plans, their conversation filled with laughter and joy.

On the other side, the head basketball coach sat in his office, the weight of the conversation heavy on his mind. He knew he had to address the situation with Brent, one of his star players, before it spiraled out of control. As Brent entered the room, the coach's expression remained composed but stern.

"Hello, coach," Brent said.

"Hey, Brent. Please take a seat. I've been wanting to chat with you."

"Sure, coach. What's up?"

"Well, Brent, I've noticed a few things happening on campus lately, and I think it's important we talk about them."

"Oh, uh, okay. What things?"

"Some concerns about you, Brent. I just want to make sure everything's okay."

"I see. Yeah, everything's fine, coach. Just some stuff going on, you know."

"I understand, Brent. But as your coach and someone who cares about you, I want to make sure you're on the right track."

Brent didn't seem happy about it and became a bit furious. "Mind your own business, coach," he snapped back, looking like he was ready to argue. "You don't know what you're talking about."

The coach didn't say anything, and he just watched as Brent stood up and left without another word. He felt really worried about Brent and what he might be getting into.

With a heavy heart, the coach realized he had to figure out how to help Brent, even if Brent didn't want to listen.

Chapter 6
Cold Carnage

THE ENGAGEMENT DAY

•••

The yacht was glided gracefully through the moonlit waters. It was beautifully adorned with twinkling fairy lights for Kiara and Mr. Romano's engagement party.

Kiara looked perfect in a red sparkling dress. She had her hair tied in a messy bun. Mr. Romano, on the other hand, looked really handsome. He wore a dark gray suit that fit him perfectly. His white shirt under the jacket and the black tie made him look classic and stylish.

A small, neat handkerchief in his pocket added a bit of fancy to his look. Together, Kiara and Mr. Romano made the party feel like a fairy tale, showing everyone what true elegance looked like on their special night. Cognac champagne was everywhere, making the party feel fancy and golden. Trays were full of lobster and Tomahawk steaks that went around among the guests.

Brent and Jay were having a great time on the fancy boat. They laughed, drank, and ate tasty food. The boat was filled with lights, and the night felt happy. Meanwhile, Jason and Erica were busy attending to the guests, ensuring everyone was having a good time. They mingled, chatted, and made sure everything was running smoothly, adding to the joyful atmosphere of the evening.

Suddenly, there was an announcement that drew everyone's attention. As the music swirled around them, Mr. Romano took a step forward, his gaze fixed lovingly on Kiara. The crowd hushed in anticipation, sensing that something special was about to happen.

With a tender smile, Mr. Romano reached for Kiara's hand, gently pulling her closer to him. "Ladies and gentlemen," he began, "I have something I'd like to share with all of you tonight."

Kiara looked up at Mr. Romano, her eyes shining with love and affection.

"From the moment I met Kiara," Mr. Romano continued, his voice filled with emotion, "I knew she was someone truly special. She has brought light and joy into my life in ways I never thought possible."

The crowd murmured in approval; their eyes fixed on the couple before them. "And so," Mr. Romano declared, his voice ringing out with sincerity, "I want to take this moment to express my love for Kiara, not just to her, but to all of you."

Tears glistened in Kiara's eyes as she listened to Mr. Romano's heartfelt words, feeling overwhelmed with love and gratitude.

"Kiara," Mr. Romano said, turning to face her fully, "you are my rock, my confidante, and my greatest love. I am so grateful to have you by my side, and I promise to cherish and honor you for all the days of my life."

With a soft gasp, Kiara threw her arms around Mr. Romano, holding him close as applause erupted around them. At that moment, surrounded by their loved ones, Kiara knew that she was exactly where she was meant to be: in the arms of the man she loved, surrounded by the love and support of those who cared for them both.

With big smiles, they put the rings on each other's fingers, showing their promise to love each other forever.

They hugged and kissed each other tightly, feeling

loved and supported by their family and friends. Kiara and Mr. Romano knew they were starting a new part of their lives together.

Kiara and Romano danced together on the floor. Everyone was excited to watch them. They held hands and moved to the music. People were happy and couldn't wait to see them dance.

Kiara and Romano made their way to the dance floor, hand in hand, their smiles radiant with happiness. As they began to sway to the music, all eyes were on them, captivated by the elegance and grace of their movements.

While dancing, Mr. Romano said, "I love you so much, Kiara. I love you more than I'm capable of saying. I've never felt this way before. I promise you I haven't. Never like this." Mr. Romano expressed his feelings.

"I love you too, more than words can express. It's a feeling I have never experienced before, and I cherish every moment with you. You are a part of my family now, Salvatore. You are truly special."

After Kiara got engaged, everyone felt really happy. Jason and Erica, Kiara's family, were thrilled to welcome Romano into their home. Romano moved in with them and started living in Kiara's house. Everyone was relieved and felt joyful to see Kiara with a partner after such a long time.

Even though Kiara was excited about getting engaged to Mr. Romano, she still had to go to her court hearings. Looking in the mirror, she thought about how her life had changed. She felt happy about her engagement and proud of her job. She dressed nicely and got ready to leave. So, after her court hearings, she checked for updates on Damien's case, who had been killed in jail.

"There's been a development in Damien's case. It appears that he was given a high dosage of drugs before his death." Ethan informed her.

Kiara's brows furrowed, "What about his laptop that we found in his apartment?"

"The forensics team is still working tirelessly on gathering evidence," he began, "But there has been a bit of progress."

Kiara's interest was piqued at the mention of progress, her curiosity driving her to lean in closer. "What have they found?" she inquired.

Ethan paused for a moment, carefully choosing his words. "It seems that Damien had maps of each American state on his laptop," he revealed, his tone tinged with intrigue. "And there's a folder containing his pictures in different clothes and hairstyles. It appears that he was using those pictures for passports to different cities and countries."

Kiara's eyes widened in surprise at the unexpected discovery. "Passports? Different cities and countries?" she repeated, trying to make sense of the new information. "But why would Damien need multiple passports? And where was he planning to go? He was an important member of the drug cartel, so why did he need different passports?"

"That's what we are trying to figure out," Ethan admitted.

"Okay, thank you, Ethan; if anything new comes up, do let me know."

"Alright, Kiara."

Kiara talked to Mr. Romano on a call about the case. "Hey, Kiara. Is everything okay? You don't sound fine." Mr. Romano asked.

Kiara sighed, "I can't seem to get Damien out of my mind. Remember I told you about him. I don't know what is happening," she remarked with concern.

"If you need to talk or if there's anything I can do,

I'm here for you, Kiara, but I don't know anything about him."

"Can you just help me a little pull the strings of people? I'm involved with you and your organization's drug cartel; don't you trust me? A man has died from the drug organization, and we should find it out."

Mr. Romano's words hung heavy in the air, his tone laced with a mixture of reassurance and resignation. "Kiara, that's none of my concern," he began, his voice measured yet tinged with a hint of unease. "If the drug mafia wants to kill someone, nobody can question that. And perhaps, neither should we."

Kiara's heart sank at Mr. Romano's words, "I understand," Kiara replied softly.

"We can't control what the drug mafia does, but we can control how we choose to live our lives," Romano said.

"Yeah, you are right. We have each other, and that's what matters most." Kiara responded. "I need to go now; I will talk to you later." She continued.

The next day, the media began pressing the authorities with inquiries about apprehending the perpetrator responsible for the string of Damien's death.

Kiara stood poised and impressive in front of the TV cameras. She appeared surprisingly relaxed under the circumstances, as if she could have done this for a living. She was very self-assured and confident whenever the situation demanded. Yet, at other times, she could be as vulnerable and afraid as the rest of us. "First, I would like to say something to all the families and friends. Please, don't give up hope. We are working on cases, and we will catch the man behind this." Kiara conveyed her message to the concerned audience.

Kiara's phone rang; she glanced at the caller ID and saw that it was her boss, Jessica. With a deep breath, Kiara answered the call, trying to compose herself. "Hey, Jessica."

Jessica's voice came through, concerned but businesslike. "Kiara, I need an update on the case. What's the progress? The press is everywhere."

"We're working on it, Jessica. It's a tough situation, and we're doing everything we can."

"Kiara, you need to understand that Damien's case is important. It's a high-profile case, and we can't afford any delay or missteps."

Kiara, however, held her ground, recognizing a

critical connection between the cases. "Jessica, I get that Damien's case is high-profile, but you need to know that everything takes time. We might find answers to Damien's case by forensic reports. The killer had managed to leave no trace."

"Kiara, I need to know each and everything about these cases," Jessica said.

"I will, Jessica. I'll do my best to get to the bottom of this. See ya!"

After an hour, Ethan and Kiara decided to check with local pharmacies regarding the Marinol and Klonopin pills that were used to kill Damien. They went from one pharmacy to another, asking pharmacists about these specific medications. However, the pharmacies had no information about them.

"We don't have those medications, and honestly, you won't find them at regular pharmacies," explained the pharmacist. "Marinol and Klonopin are usually prescribed by doctors, and you'd typically get them from a hospital or someone working in the healthcare field."

Kiara, eager for any lead, asked the pharmacist, "Can you name any hospitals or healthcare professionals who might have access to Marinol and Klonopin?"

After a moment of thought, the pharmacist provided a list, "Well, you might want to check with University Hospital, Dr. Martinez's clinic, and City Medical Center. These places have professionals who could have these medications."

They headed to Dr. Martinez's clinic and City Medical Center to learn more about the medications. When they arrived at Dr. Martinez's clinic, they were informed that he wasn't available.

Kiara sighed, "Let's check Miami's Medical Center. We need to find out more about Marinol and Klonopin."

At Miami's Medical Center, they approached the front desk. Kiara spoke to the receptionist, "Hi, we're detectives investigating a case related to certain medications. Can we speak to someone who can help us understand more about Marinol and Klonopin?"

"I'll check if someone is available. Please have a seat."

While waiting, Ethan whispered to Kiara, "Let's hope they have some answers. We need a breakthrough in this case."

A nurse, Ms. Rodriguez, came to greet them. "How can I assist you?" she asked.

Kiara explained, "We're looking into a case involving Marinol and Klonopin. Any information you can provide about who prescribes or has access to these medications would be very helpful."

Ms. Rodriguez nodded, "I can't give out patient information, but I can guide you to the pharmacy department or talk to the hospital pharmacist. They might have more information about the distribution of these medications." Ethan thanked her, and they headed towards the pharmacy department.

"These drugs are usually prescribed for specific medical conditions. Mr. Lopez can check our records for any unusual prescriptions or patterns."

"That would be great. We're trying to connect the dots in a case related to these medications."

Mr. Lopez, the pharmacist, took a moment to review the records before turning to Kiara and Ethan with a thoughtful expression. "I've checked our records, and I can confirm that Marinol and Klonopin, on their own, don't have the potential to kill people. However, their constant misuse can certainly lead to serious health issues."

Intrigued, Kiara asked, "How is that possible?

What are the risks associated with these medications?"

Mr. Lopez explained, "Marinol contains an active ingredient found in the cannabis plant. It's prescribed to manage certain conditions, but some individuals may misuse it. Because of this, some people have reported experiencing side effects typically related to THC, such as euphoria or hallucinations."

Ethan, absorbing the information, inquired further, "And what about Klonopin? How can it be harmful?"

Mr. Lopez continued, "Klonopin belongs to a class of drugs called benzodiazepines. While it's effective in treating anxiety and seizures when used as prescribed, excessive or prolonged use can lead to dependency and severe withdrawal symptoms. In extreme cases, misuse can indeed have fatal consequences."

Kiara nodded, realizing the gravity of the situation. "So, if someone intentionally gives a high dose or mixes these medications without proper medical supervision, it could be lethal?"

Mr. Lopez nodded in agreement, "Yes, exactly. Intentional misuse or a combination of these drugs, especially without proper medical guidance, can pose serious risks."

"Mr. Lopez, do you currently have Marinol and Klonopin in stock?"

Mr. Lopez furrowed his brow before responding, "We used to have them, but they were stolen from the pharmacy. It happened about a week ago. We received a stock of these pills, but when we went to retrieve them, they were nowhere to be found."

Kiara's eyes widened in surprise. "Stolen? How is that possible?"

Mr. Lopez sighed, "It's concerning, indeed. We've been investigating internally, but so far, we haven't been able to trace the person responsible for the theft."

Kiara, contemplating the information about the stolen pills, voiced her thoughts, "This could be an inside job. It might be someone from the hospital, perhaps a nursing staff, a doctor, or even a pharmacist."

Mr. Lopez, hesitant to suspect his colleagues, responded, "It's hard to believe that our own employees would do something like this. We have a strict system in place, and everyone is aware of the consequences of such actions."

"We can't rule anyone out at this point. We need

to consider all possibilities. Who else has access to this pharmacy apart from you?"

Mr. Lopez sighed, "Well, there's the cleaning staff who come in during the night for routine cleaning. Other than that, only authorized personnel have access, and that includes a few senior nurses and doctors who might need medications for emergency cases."

Ethan, adding to the discussion, asked, "Is there a log or record of entries? We need to know who was in the pharmacy around the time when the pills went missing."

Mr. Lopez nodded, "We maintain a logbook. I can provide you with a copy, and you can check the entries around that time."

"Do you have any security footage or any leads that might help us identify the thief?" Ethan asked.

Mr. Lopez nodded, "We do have cameras, but unfortunately, the footage from that time is missing. It's as if someone deliberately tampered with it."

"We need all the information you have. Every detail might be crucial in solving this case. Can we access the remaining footage and any other records related to the stolen pills?"

The revelation of the stolen medications marked

another significant turning point for Kiara and Ethan.

Kiara, flipping through the pages, remarked, "This could be the break we've been waiting for. Let's see who was in the pharmacy around the time the pills went missing."

Kiara, determined to connect the dots, turned to Mr. Lopez and said, "I'll need you to email us the logbook details. Let's head to the footage room and see if we can spot anything unusual."

In the dimly lit room filled with rows of screens, Kiara and Ethan joined the camera handlers. Ethan asked, "Have you noticed anything unusual in the vicinity lately?"

The camera handler, shaking his head, replied, "No, nothing out of the ordinary. Everything has been routine."

"Let's start with the footage from a few weeks back, around October 15. That's when the pills were stolen."

As they played back the footage, the screens flickered to life, revealing the comings and goings within the hospital. Kiara's eyes scanned the screen until they landed on a figure entering the pharmacy late at night. The person was wearing a white coat with a mask and stethoscope around their neck – unmistakably a doctor.

Ethan, pointing at the screen, exclaimed, "There! That's a doctor entering the pharmacy. Let's see who it is."

"That's Doctor Rodriguez in the footage. He's allowed to go inside."

Kiara, processing the information, questioned, "But could he have been involved in the theft of the medications? Where's he now?"

The camera handler responded, "He's on holiday and will be back the day after tomorrow."

On the next day, at midnight, something terrible happened. Carol was found DEAD in her bathtub. Her body looked purple, and her face was very pale. The first person to see her was Dan, her husband.

Dan quickly called the police, and they came to take Carol's body. The house seemed usual – but there were two coffee cups on the table. The rest of everything else in the house was in the right place. Their kids weren't at home that day; they were staying at Carol's sister's house. Carol was alone at home that day. She wasn't even at work.

"I can't believe this happened to my Carol. Why

her?" Dan sobbed in front of the police officers.'

"We're so sorry for your loss, Dan. We need to ask you some questions." The Police Officer asked.

"Okay, I'll try," Dan said with teary eyes.

"Were you the one who found her?"

"Yeah, I came home, and she... she was in the bathtub." Dan nodded.

"Did you notice anything unusual?"

"No, everything seemed normal," Dan said, sniffling.

"Were there any problems or arguments recently between you and Carol?"

"No, nothing. It was a regular day. Our kids are with her sister today."

"Do you remember anything more? How has she been behaving in the past few days? Was there any change?"

"Yeah, Carol was going through something, but she wasn't comfortable sharing it with me."

"What was that? Did you ask her?"

"Yeah, I tried, but she wasn't feeling well. She seemed uninterested in everything, not even about me or our kids. She kept hearing strange noises from our backyard, insisting someone attacked her on the terrace, but it turned out to be just a bat at night. She got hurt and stayed home."

"Do you think that there might be something related to her work?"

"She stopped going to work. She was really stressed about a case involving Judge Kiara. They had a lot of arguments about it."

"Why? What happened?"

"Carol thought something was off with the case, but Judge Kiara disagreed. They argued about it, and Carol just couldn't handle the stress anymore."

"And you didn't do anything, Mr. Dan, to help your wife?"

"It was a professional rivalry between Kiara and Carol. My wife was a sweet and kind woman. It was something between her and Kiara. But I suggested her therapy to get some help."

"Thank you, Mr. Dan. We'll do our best to find out what happened. If you remember anything or need support, let us know."

"Thank you, officer. I just can't believe she's gone." Dan said while crying.

The news of Carol's death spread, and the media began asking, "Who killed Judge Carol?"

Everybody was talking about Carol's death. People were discussing it everywhere, from talking quietly in cafes to reading about it in newspapers and social media. Everyone wanted to know who had done something so bad to Judge Carol. Everyone wanted Justice!!!

In the aftermath of Carol's tragic demise, the autopsy report came and revealed a grim reality. The forensic examination discloses that she succumbed to poisoning, a deliberate act that abruptly ended her life.

The belief spread that Kiara might have given her poison, given their professional rivalry. On TV and social media, the news about Kiara being accused of killing Carol was everywhere.

But Kiara was nowhere to be found, completely unreachable. She wasn't answering calls, messages, or meeting in person. Kiara didn't come home, and nobody knew anything about her, not Jason, Erica, Mr. Madders, or Mr. Romano. All were clueless!

Kiara watched an interview with her boss on TV, expressing condolences for the loss of Judge Carol Hidding. The announcement followed, stating they were now searching for Judge Kiara Tierson.

WHAT! YOU BITCH! Kiara exclaimed to herself, shocked and distressed by the false accusations.

Finally, Kiara meets with Jessica, her boss. The security guard informed her, "Judge Kiara is here to meet you." "Send her inside."

"Alright, Kiara? What's been going on?" asked Jessica. "Why haven't you been answering my calls? What the fuck has been happening? Did you see the news? Everyone is asking about you, Judge Kiara. Where have you been? Hiding from the police? People are saying you killed Carol because you argued with her over the case." Jessica questioned aggressively.

"Do you have any evidence regarding me?" Kiara asked.

"Wow!!! And people will believe you? Do you think this? So what are you, huh? You will kill people, and nobody will question you? Everything is on the news."

"You've gone mad, Jessica. Taking matters into your own hands is not the way to go. You DO NOT have any proof."

I need justice for Carol, and I will do the justice." Jessica exclaimed.

"Do whatever you want to do, Jessica; she's dead, and I don't care," Kiara said and left the office.

•••

In the days that followed, the police persisted in their search for evidence implicating Kiara, but despite their efforts, concrete proof remained elusive. Frustration mounted within law enforcement circles as they struggled to build a compelling case against Kiara.

The very building where Kiara diligently worked was engulfed in a cataclysmic explosion. The cops moved faster in the semidarkness of the building as if nothing could stop them from killing Judge Kiara.

They found the doorway out at last. There was no lock, no doorknob. They had blown it away. The stairway was clear; at least, it looked that way. Everything was surging out of control; many precious lives were lost. There was blood everywhere. It was a wild, jubilant scene, one that is hard to forget.

All eyes were on Kiara now. But by a stroke of fate, Kiara was not present in the building at the time.

The targeted attack had not been random; it was a ruthless attempt to eliminate Judge Kiara.

On that fateful night, as darkness enveloped the city, Jessica's phone rang, breaking the silence with an eerie intensity. An unknown number flashed on the screen.

"Extraordinary time to be alive, right?" The voice on the other end belonged to none other than Judge Kiara, her tone dripping with sarcasm. "Aren't you worried about me, Jessica? Look, I'm still alive."

Jessica's lips curled into a sinister smirk as she listened to Kiara's taunts. "I will find you and kill you," she retorted.

"But you have already killed several precious lives because of me. I have so many nightmarish images in my mind now. So, how will you face the media and people? Do you need any of my help?" Her words cut through the air like a razor, leaving Jessica unsettled.

"Run for your life," Jessica replied, her anger simmering just beneath the surface.

"I will try not to call. You rest up, though," she quipped before abruptly ending the call.

Chapter 7
Blood Bound

"Hurry up! Hurry up! Transport the guns and drugs in the yacht before sunrise!"

The noise of drug crates being moved out on the hard floor bounced around the big warehouse. Every second counted as everyone worked feverishly to complete the task at hand.

Judge Kiara stood nearby; her expression focused as she observed the operation unfold. Judge Kiara and Mr. Romano were in charge, wearing black suits and telling everyone what to do. The team listened to them carefully. Kiara looked serious but calm.

"Make sure those boxes are on the yachts properly," Judge Kiara said firmly.

She moved around confidently, giving orders. She would do anything for Mr. Romano, even if it meant breaking the law.

The allure of danger and power was intoxicating, and Judge Kiara found herself falling deeper into a world she never thought she would be a part of. Her feelings for Mr. Romano clouded her judgment, blurring the lines between right and wrong.

The guns and drugs were worth millions of dollars, a fortune waiting to be transported to various parts of the United States.

These drugs were more than just merchandise; they were the key to a life of luxury and influence. The guns were the best you could find, all shiny and new. They were made to be super strong and dangerous, better than any before them. Each gun was built to be as effective and deadly as possible.

Among them were AR-15 rifles, AK-47s, Glock handguns, and Remington shotguns. These were all top-of-the-line firearms known for their power and accuracy. With advanced features and high-tech designs, they were ready for action whenever they were needed.

The members of the drug cartel hustled, their hands moving swiftly as they dealt with the large boxes.

Meanwhile, Mr. Romano took a moment to

approach Judge Kiara.

"Without you, none of this would be possible," Mr. Romano said.

"I can do anything for you," she replied, "We all have to play our part."

"I appreciate that, Kiara, and I love you more than anything else," he replied.

"I love you too. Now, let's not forget the risks involved in what we're doing. We need to be very careful." Kiara said.

"Come on, team, let's pick up the pace! We've got just an hour left," Mr. Romano commanded. "There are still crates left in the trucks and the warehouse."

Meanwhile, Judge Kiara made her way into the luxurious interior of the yacht. "Wow," she breathed, "This yacht is exquisite."

Her eyes swept over the plush furnishings and gleaming fixtures, marveling at the sheer decadence of it all.

"No one will ever know that under the confines of this extravagant vessel lay millions of dollars' worth of drugs and ammunition." She said to herself.

With a sense of satisfaction, Judge Kiara inspected

every corner of the yacht, ensuring that their illicit cargo was securely stowed away.

When the last truck left, Judge Kiara smiled at Mr. Romano. "Good job tonight," she said.

"We did it," he muttered.

Together, they took a moment to praise the efforts of everyone who had worked tirelessly to ensure the success of their operation. Each member of their team had played a vital role, and their dedication had not gone unnoticed. "Great job, everyone; you will be rewarded soon." Mr. Romano announced. "Now leave this place as soon as possible."

The yacht now sailed away; Judge Kiara and Mr. Romano kissed passionately once everyone was gone and made their way back home.

A FEW DAYS LATER

●●●

Kiara received a phone call that changed everything. The person on the other end was Ethan, who told her something very difficult to hear – Brent had been killed. As she listened, shock and sadness washed over her like a wave.

"No, this can't be true! My son can't die. There must be some mistake. Brent can't be dead." Her voice trembled with fear and tears in her eyes.

"I understand this is hard to believe, but he is your son. We found his college ID, and he was discovered on the football field of his college. We need you to come here."

Kiara, her voice choked with sorrow and disbelief, responded, "No, no, this can't be true. Brent can't be gone."

Kiara, gripping the steering wheel tightly, drove her car frantically towards Brent's college. Tears streamed down her face, blurring the road ahead. The weight of grief and disbelief pressed heavily on her heart. As she arrived at the place where the tragic incident occurred, she couldn't contain the anguish within.

In a voice strained with sorrow, she cried out, "No, Brent, no! This can't be real!" The scream echoed the depths of her pain and shattered emotions. The world seemed to stand still, consumed by the overwhelming grief that engulfed Kiara as she faced the harsh reality of Brent's death.

"WHO DID THIS? WHO IS THIS, TELL ME.

WHO KILLED MY SON?" She said furiously.

"He was shot twice in his head. We asked a few questions from the students, but we couldn't find any traces of the murderer. We're trying our best to figure out what happened." Ethan explained.

"I NEED THAT BASTARD!!! HE KILLED MY SON, MY BABY." Kiara yelled with tears.

Ethan, trying to offer comfort, gently said, "Kiara, I know this is hard, but you need to be strong. We'll do everything we can to find the person responsible. I promise you that we will get to the bottom of this very soon."

Many people came to say goodbye to Brent at his funeral – teachers, friends, and his teammates. Everyone looked very sad. Romano, Jason, and Brock (Jason's best friend) were the pallbearers at Brent's funeral. But Jay wasn't there. Kiara, though she cried, stayed strong. The atmosphere was heavy with sadness as they all tried to come to terms with the fact that Brent was gone.

Kiara was still in shock, but she didn't show it in her eyes. Jason was very upset, having a hard time accepting what had happened. The sadness hung in the air, and each of them was finding it tough to say goodbye to Brent.

THE NEXT DAY

●●●

Bang! Bang!

Kiara descended into a world of chaos by enacting revenge on those who wronged her. She pulls out her pistol and shoots the enemies before confronting The Actual Cartel Mafia.

As Kiara was involved in running the group, dealing with drugs, guns, and money, and planning hits for UNC and Judge, she found out UNC had something to do with Brent's killing. This made her really angry and feeling betrayed. So, she decided to take matters into her own hands and began killing UNC members.

Fueled by fury and a thirst for revenge, Kiara stormed one of their drug spots, unleashing her wrath upon those responsible for Brent's death.

While driving, Kiara shoots at a bunch of assassins, and, well, she also hits a few with her Range Rover. Her mind was focused on Ramos Diego. Catch Him, Kill Him.

She did the initial blast, and it was a sharp, piercing noise, quickly overtaken by the resonating rumble that seemed to linger in the air, leaving behind an eerie silence in its wake. Bullets zipped through the air, tearing through crates and sending shards of wood and debris in all directions.

In the shadowy alley, Kiara's grip tightened around the cold steel of her weapon. She was out of her car now.

She held Heckler & Koch HK416 and unleashed a barrage of bullets through the alley. Kiara feels like a predator, stalking her prey and attacking them with perfect headshots and deadly takedowns.

Kiara goes in guns blazing, killing anyone that gets in her way. Although she was looking out for Ramos, but she stabbed a knife in Damien's eyes, who dared to protect him. He wasn't dead in the jail. They faked his death. This led to an all-out street war.

Kiara's attire consists of a well-fitted, jet-black suit made from premium materials like wool or cashmere.

The suit's design ensures flexibility for unrestricted movement, particularly during intense combat sequences. Additionally, she complements the ensemble with a bulletproof vest to protect her from the bullets.

Ethan was with Kiara, shooting the other half of the guys. He broke the protocol and helped her.

Adjacent to the alley stood a warehouse where Ramos had sought refuge. He sprinted through the streets of Mexico, racing onto the road. Kiara pursued him, and he fired a shot backward, narrowly missing her. Kiara, driven by a vengeful rage, also killed anyone who came near her. Kiara fought really hard. She was good at shooting accurately from a distance and fighting up close. Judge Kiara crouched behind the overturned table, her heart pounding in sync with the rapid bursts of gunfire echoing through the dimly lit warehouse. She took down her enemies quickly and was tough in a face-to-face fight.

She chased after Ramos, and he hurriedly entered the Royal Mexican club.

They had a brief hand-to-hand struggle, and when he tries to escape, the fight moves upstairs in the club, and everything becomes chaotic. The dance floor is thumped with loud music and colorful lights. Kiara has to fight through a lot of bad guys who keep coming.

Kiara sprinted up the narrow staircase, her breath quickening as she pursued the man through the dimly lit corridor.

There It WAS, Ramos Diego.

He glanced over his shoulder and saw no way to

be out of life and death race.

"I just can't wait for the whole thing to be over, and I guess you couldn't wait for it to be over either, Kiara muttered to him angrily.

He chuckled nervously and said. "Look, lady, we can talk about this. Maybe we can work something out, you know?"

"Talk? After all you've put me through? You son of a Bit*h, you took everything from me."

"I didn't think it would come to this. I just needed a way out, you know?"

"At the expense of innocent lives? You've got a lot to answer for."

He swallowed hard and said. "Look, I didn't mean for things to go this far. It just spiraled out of control."

"There's a price to pay for the choices we make. Yours just caught up with you." She said aggressively while holding a gun in her hands.

"What do you gain by taking me down? A few medals and accolades in exchange for the life of your own child, perhaps?" he taunted, a sly grin playing on his face.

"You took my son away from me, you bastard.'

"Huh? Come on, I don't care."

"You fucker!" she sneered and rushed.

As she rushed, Ramos swung a powerful right. Kiara met him halfway and lashed him out with his own right. Her punch was faster, and it caught the big man flush, but Ramos took it on the mouth, spat blood, and hurled him into the dust with such force that a cloud of dust arose.

The big renegade jerked up a stiff thumb, trying for Kiara's eye, but she rolled her head away and swung a left to the wind, and then a driving right but ripped her ear skin, starting a shower of blood.

Kiara now charged again and caught him with two long swings on the head. His skull roaring with pain and dizziness, Ramos braced himself and started to swing in a blind fury, both hands going with every ounce of power he could muster.

Kiara shifted her attack with lightning speed. He missed a right and, following it in with the weight of his body, slid his arm around Ramos thick neck, grabbed the wrist with her left hand, jerked up his feet, and sat down hard, trying to break his neck.

But the big renegade knew all the tricks, and as Kiara's feet flew up, Ramos hurled his weight forward and to the left, falling with his body half across the stairs. It broke the hold, and they both rolled free.

There was a pause for a moment. Kiara came to her feet, and Ramos, catlike in his speed, lashed out with a wicked kick for his blood-battered head.

Ramos was bloody and battered now, yet he kept coming, his breath wheezing. Kiara stabbed a left into his face, set himself, and whipped up a right uppercut to the body. He gasped.

Kiara circled, then smashed him in the body with another right, then another and another. His jaw was hanging open now. Although Kiara's face was battered and bleeding from a dozen cuts and abrasions, she still kept on fighting.

Ramos collapses to the floor. Then she hacks his head off. It falls to the floor, does a half-roll, and comes to rest, staring straight up at the ceiling. He's DEAD!!!

His death wasn't so quick, and it was done with gravitas or over-the-top stunts. Then again, maybe that's exactly what he deserves.

Kiara staggered slightly, then ambled over to the watering trough, bending her head to immerse it.

The next day, Kiara destroyed the buildings

belonging to the Cartel Mafia. Kiara targeted the Cartel Mafia's hideout, including their drug storage facility and command center.

On the yacht, Kiara killed Alejandro Torres, another relative of Mr. Romano. He came straight at her, and she dodged left. But he was ready for that maneuver, and he landed a right hook in the center of her stomach. She came up off her feet and went down on her back. Then, it was about choosing to live or choose to die. She chose to live. Rolled over twice, pushed with her hands, and levered herself upright. Jumped back and sideways and dodged a straight drive that would have killed her, but she survived.

He was fast, but he wasn't talented. Kiara got an elbow in his face. It cracked his nose. It should have punched it out the back of his head. But at least it started bleeding. He bled REAL HARD!!!

His mouth was open because of the blood in his nose. She wound up and let go with a cigarette punch. It's a bar fight trick that she learned long ago.

"Enough of fighting now, right? Let's just throw you into hell."

"Please let me go, he begged her."

"You killed my son!!! You son of a bit*h."

She took out her pistol and shot him. He's DEAD TOO!

Kiara took out a hand grenade from her pocket, her eyes determined. She walked up to the yacht and removed the pin from the grenade, then threw it onto the boat and ran away.

BOOM! The grenade exploded, making a loud noise. Smoke filled the air, and the yacht was all broken. Kiara stood there, showing she wouldn't let anyone harm her without fighting back.

By the third day, Kiara had confronted the drug cartel head-on. She aimed and fired at many members, even Mr. Romano's cousins and friends. Buildings and centers were not spared either; she detonated explosives, destroying them in her relentless pursuit.

But Mr. Romano sees that Kiara can't be stopped, and she can hurt anyone who tries to get in her way. She didn't talk to anyone; she was off doing the job of ending the lives of the people who took her son away.

After killing numerous ruthless criminals, the President of the US decides that Judge Kiara's courage deserves recognition. He appoints her as a Justice on the

Supreme Court. The public praises her for her bravery in taking down drug dealers, and she becomes a symbol of strength and justice.

After two weeks, Kiara was home exhausted. Her face bears the marks of weariness. Her story has spread across the news, and people everywhere applauded her strength and resilience, but they didn't know that Kiara was killing them because of her own purpose.

"Mom, you're on the news everywhere! They're all talking about how strong you are!" Jason said while hugging her.

"Thanks, Jason."

"You're like a superhero, Mom! I'm so proud of you."

"I just want a safer world for you. I can't lose you." Kiara said.

Mr. Romano noticed her condition, and they shared a heartfelt hug before heading inside the house together. Kiara was overjoyed to be back home.

"Are you okay, Kiara? Why didn't you tell me you were going alone to deal with them?"

"I didn't want you to get hurt in any way. I have lost Brent. I can't lose anyone." Kiara responded.

"I understand, but we're meant to be together. We should face this together, Kiara. Don't leave me alone. Promise me?"

"Yes, I promise," she said.

At night, Mr. Romano couldn't sleep. He kept thinking about what Kiara did and how she killed many people. Even though he was upset, he couldn't leave her. Then, he got a call from someone, and he left to receive the call.

"Hey, I told you not to call me. Give me some time, and I will get back to you."

"Don't you know what Judge Kiara did? She killed our men, and she blew up our places. She's a bit*h. Kill her and come back to us."

"I can't stop thinking about what Kiara did. She's taken so many lives. I will deal with it." The caller on the other said.

"I can't give you another chance, Mr. Romano. Enough now!!! That woman did terrible things to us. She might not know what she's getting into."

"I can't just leave her alone, though. Please trust me, I will do something." Mr. Romano said with concern.

"Hurry up, the clock is ticking. Things might get

messier than you think." The caller said and ended the call.

"Who was it?" A voice came from behind; it was Kiara asking Mr. Romano, with whom he was talking on the call. Mr. Romano said, "Just a friend, I have some unfinished business with him."

She said, "You sure, right?"

"Yeah, just some old matters to settle."

"Old matters, huh? You know you can trust me, right?"

"Of course, Kiara. You're my partner in everything."

"Just be careful. I don't want anything to happen to you." Kiara said.

"Yes, my love, nothing will happen to me." Mr. Romano said. They both went into the room, holding each other closely.

The next day, Kiara couldn't shake off the desire for revenge against Brent's killers again. She wanted to kill everyone. Determination etched on her face, she reached out to Ethan, hoping for progress in their pursuit.

"Hey, Ethan, any leads on where those rest of the killers are hiding?" Kiara asked.

"Yeah, Kiara. They're near a small town in Mexico.

We'll have to travel there with proper ammunition; they might be armed with an array of guns."

"We can't let them get away with what they did to Brent. Let's go, Ethan. We'll finish this."

"Just be prepared, Kiara. This won't be easy." Ethan warned.

"I'm always prepared. Wait for me, and I will be there. Let's finish this business once and for all," Kiara declared with determined resolve.

Kiara left a message for Jason and Mr. Romano explaining her departure; she wrote:

Something Urgent Came Up, and I Will Be Back Soon!

Kiara was again gone. Mr. Romano was aware that she had gone to take matters into her own hands again, felt a surge of anger, but found himself unable to take any further action.

Chapter 8
Lies and Deceit

Kiara was back at her home. She received a text from Mr. Romano saying that he was going to be a bit late this evening; he had to take a client out for a drink. Kiara was getting ready for an evening walk. She was in her room. The light was just gorgeous, a rich orange glow filling the house, turning suddenly blue-grey when the sun went behind a cloud. She had the curtains pulled halfway across to stop the room from getting too hot, so she went to open them, and that's when she saw a man wearing black clothes and a mask, standing on the opposite side of the road, looking at their house.

Kiara opened her eyes and looked around clearly. The road was very quiet: just one woman walking a few hundred yards off, no one else. No cars driving past, no children shouting, only a very faint siren in the distance. The sun slid behind a cloud, and she felt cold.

Meanwhile, upstairs in her room, Kiara's mind raced with questions. Who could he be, and why was he here? Could it be connected to Brent? Her mind screamed. Fueled by adrenaline and fear, she flew across the landing, her eyes fixed on the retreating form.

She ran up the stairs and towards him, thinking that he might be someone linked to UNC or he might be any member. She ran swiftly, but when she reached the opposite end, he was gone. Panic mingled with confusion. Where had he gone? Had she imagined it all? But she came back home. When Mr. Romano was home, Kiara didn't say a word about this black mask man.

At midnight, Kiara stirred from her sleep, her eyes blinking open in the dimness of the room. As she adjusted to the darkness, she realized that Mr. Romano wasn't beside her in bed. A sense of unease crept over her as she scanned the room, searching for any sign of his presence. But there was nothing – no sound, no movement, just the quiet stillness of the night. She tried to think back to earlier in the evening when she saw a man outside of their house.

Kiara frowned and sat up in bed, feeling worried. She wondered where Mr. Romano could be at this late hour. Was something wrong? As these thoughts raced through her mind, she started to feel anxious. She got out of bed quietly, walking across the room with bare feet. The floor felt cool beneath her toes. Concern knotted her stomach as she searched downstairs, and Mr. Romano was nowhere to be found.

The silence felt heavy, amplifying the unanswered calls on her phone. Venturing outside, she scanned the familiar surroundings, worry etching lines on her brow. The crisp night air held no sign of him, just the rustle of unseen leaves and the distant hum of crickets. But then, a sound cut through the quietude - a whisper, faint yet unmistakably Mr. Romano's voice. There was someone with him. But Kiara couldn't recognize the voice. It seemed to come from somewhere beyond the garden's edge, beyond the pool of light cast by the porch lamp. Curiosity and concern battled within her. Should she investigate? What dangers might lurk in the shadows? Taking a deep breath, she steeled her nerves and followed the whispering deeper into the unknown, guided by an unwavering hope of finding Mr. Romano safe and sound. Slowly, carefully, she crept closer. Her heart hammered in her chest as she saw Mr. Romano in the darkness, talking to the same creepy guy in black and a mask. Mr. Romano looked super mad, even more than she'd ever seen him! The other guy looked even angrier like he could explode! What was going on here?

"I don't want to talk about Brent. He's dead now, and killing him wasn't easy," said Mr. Romano. "I've got to think of staying alive."

"Most of our men are DEAD now!!! What you care is about yourself???" The man said aggressively.

"I gotta live; otherwise, you will be killed, too. We need her for our plans. Do you understand that?"

"We want you to silence her just like you silenced Brent. Shut her mouth and hands. She's killing our men." The man said.

"I will deal with her, and we still have men with us; just go and check on them." Mr. Romano said.

"All right," said the other man. "I'm going out to check on my men in half an hour anyway."

Kiara had no idea what they were talking about; however, it seemed to be all connected, something linked to Brent's death. "They're using me?" she croaked, her voice barely a whisper. She came a bit near, and it was that BLACK MASK MAN!

Fear gnawed at her. She wouldn't be intimidated. "Why did they kill him? These Bastards!"

Kiara came back and sat in her dimly lit room, her mind swirling with conflicting emotions. She had noticed a change in Mr. Romano, her fiancé. He seemed distant, distracted, haunted by something she couldn't quite grasp. But now, everything has become clear.

Kiara's world shattered as the realization hit her like a freight train. The fragments of suspicion and unease she had been carrying suddenly coalesced into a devastating truth: Mr. Romano had something to do with Brent's death; their engagement was a facade masking a sinister secret.

Tears streamed down her cheeks uncontrollably as she grappled with the betrayal and heartbreak. How could the man she loved, the one she had planned a future with, be involved in such a heinous act?

Kiara's head was filled with memories, but they felt different now. The happy times they had shared, the fun they had together, the things they promised each other—all of it seemed fake now. She couldn't even stand to look at the ring on her finger, a sign of love that wasn't real.

Kiara loved Mr. Romano, even though he hurt her.

She felt angry and wanted to hurt him back and kill him right on his head, but she stopped herself from acting on those feelings. She knew that acting impulsively wouldn't make things better.

On the same night, when Mr. Romano came back to his room, Kiara confronted him. She demanded answers, her heart breaking with every word that passed between them.

"Mr. Romano, we need to talk," Kiara demanded for quick answers.

"Kiara? What are you doing so late?" Mr. Romano asked.

"Who was that man in black? Where did you go?" Kiara asked.

"Kiara, please, it's not what you think. He was just a friend."

"Then tell me! Tell me where you went! Did you have something to do with Brent's death?" Kiara asked in a high tone.

"No, Kiara, of course not. How could you even think that of me? I loved Brent like a son."

Kiara said with desperation in her voice, "I don't know what to believe anymore, Mr. Romano. I saw the pain in your eyes tonight, the guilt. You have to tell me the truth."

"Kiara, you have to trust me. I would never hurt Brent. He was everything to me."

"Then why won't you tell me where you were tonight? Why won't you be honest with me?"

Mr. Romano said, struggling for words. "I... I can't. You wouldn't understand."

"I can't do this anymore, Mr. Romano. I can't stay with someone who won't be honest with me. I'm sorry, but I have to leave." Kiara yelled with anger.

Mr. Romano with a voice breaking, said, "Kiara, please don't go. I need you. I love you."

"I'm sorry, Mr. Romano. But love shouldn't be built on lies. Leave my house right now. Goodbye!!!"

Silence fills the room as Kiara turns and walks away, leaving Mr. Romano alone with his thoughts and his secrets. But the truth was undeniable, the evidence damning. He couldn't hide from the accusations, couldn't escape the weight of his actions.

And so, with a heavy heart and tears in her eyes, Kiara made the agonizing decision to break off their engagement. She couldn't stay with a man who had betrayed her trust, who had shattered her heart into a million irreparable pieces.

Mr. Romano didn't say anything in response to Kiara's accusations now. He simply turned and walked out of her home, leaving her heartbroken and alone. She felt the emptiness consume her. The pain was overwhelming, a raw ache that gnawed at her soul. And though her heart may be broken, Kiara knew that she would survive, and she had to kill the drug cartel people more.

Kiara felt really sad. She understood that Carol had tried to tell her about Romano and the Cartel gang, but now Carol was gone, and it was because of Kiara's mistake. Kiara blamed herself for not listening and felt guilty for Carol's death.

THE FOLLOWING DAY

•••

It was just starting to rain when Kiara got there, with not a soul in sight, but she parked the car and walked around the graveyard anyway. She found her grave right in the furthest corner, almost hidden under a line of firs. It was Carol's grave.

You would never know that she was there unless

you knew to go looking. The headstone marker bears her name and the dates of her life. At least now her grave is properly marked; she's not all alone.

Kiara sat alone at Carol's grave, tears streaming down her cheeks as she gazed at the simple headstone marking her friend's final resting place. I'm sorry Carol!

Memories of their laughter and shared moments flooded her mind. She was missing her a lot. She was also missing her son, Brent.

The weight of grief pressed heavily upon Kiara's shoulders as she struggled to get better. I hate myself for crying, and it's so pathetic. But I feel exhausted; these past few weeks have been so hard on me. But then I think, this happens sometimes, doesn't it? People you have a history with won't let you go, and as hard as you might try, you can't disentangle yourself, can't set yourself free. Maybe after a while, you just stop trying. Kiara thought.

Brent's final resting place was also near the cemetery, not far from where Kiara was standing at Carol's grave. She walked, and in the quiet stillness of the cemetery, Kiara found solace in the presence of Brent's memory.

She whispered words of love and longing to the

silent tombstone. "Brent, she began, her voice trembling with emotion. "I miss you more than words can express. You were always there for me through the good times and the bad. I wish you were still here with me, baby, sharing in my joys and my sorrows. Brent, my sweet son," she continued, her voice breaking with sorrow. "I can't believe you're gone. I never got the chance to say goodbye, to tell you how much I love you. I will cherish every memory we shared, every laugh, every smile. You were taken from me too soon, and my heart aches with the emptiness of your absence. But even as I mourn, I find comfort in knowing that you're together now, watching over me from above. Rest in peace, my dear Brent. Your love will live on in my heart forever." With tears streaming down her cheeks, Kiara placed a bouquet at each grave, a small token of her enduring love and affection.

Then, she drives back to her home, and she starts thinking about how nice it would be to sit in a leather armchair in their cozy with a glass of wine and everyone sitting in front of her – Brent, Jason, Erica, and Mr. Romano. But it was all her imagination; in reality, everything had been shattered.

As the sun went down, Kiara felt ready to finish

what she had started. She called Ethan, telling him it was time to deal with unfinished business with the UNC members. They both flew to Mexico again. Ethan told her they had found some more drug cartel members and a person who had been making Carol's life miserable.

"We found the bad guy. His name is Luis Rivera. We will find this man in La Fiesta Loca Bar." Ethan told her.

"Let's go and get them," Kiara said firmly.

Kiara got mad at the thought of Carol suffering. She quickly put on her black fighting clothes and went to deal with them. Together, they went to confront the person causing all the trouble. There were more to go. Kiara was determined, and Ethan was right there with her, ready to face whatever came their way.

In Mexico, Kiara and Ethan wasted no time. They combed through streets and alleys.

As Kiara and Ethan stepped into the dimly lit bar, the noisy atmosphere suddenly quieted down as if everyone was expecting them. The air smelled strong of tequila, and you could hear Mexican music playing softly in the background, making everything feel tense.

Kiara and Ethan didn't hesitate. They had guns

with them. They moved quickly and with a clear purpose through the crowded bar. They didn't waste a moment and got into fights with some people there, showing they were very skilled and determined.

Amidst all the chaos, Kiara looked around, and then, she spotted him – Luis Rivera, sitting calmly with a glass of wine. Kiara's eyes met his, and it was clear that something horrible was about to happen between them. Ethan stood close by, ready to help Kiara if she needed it.

Luis Rivera's expression turned angry, and he seemed to grow larger with rage. Suddenly, he lunged at Kiara without any second thought, swinging his right arm in a wide roundhouse strike. She swiftly stepped aside and ducked under his arm, then quickly spun around. As he recoiled, she found herself closer to the guns than he was. Panic flashed in her eyes as he charged at her again, repeating the same move. Once more, she sidestepped and ducked, returning us to their starting positions. However, he was starting to breathe harder than her, showing signs of exhaustion.

He stood there, panting. Kiara was warming up nicely. She was beginning to feel she had some kind of a chance. He was a very poor fighter. Lots of very big guys are bad at fighting.

Either their sheer size is so intimidating it stops fights from ever starting in the first place, or else it lets them win everyone directly after their first punch lands. Either way, they don't get much practice. They don't develop much finesse. Kiara figured he had weight-lifted himself right out of the frame.

She blew him a kiss, taunting him. He lunged at her like a bulldozer, charging through the air with force. She dodged to the left and countered with an elbow to his face, but he managed to land a hit with his left hand, sending her staggering sideways as if she weighed nothing.

Regaining her balance, she narrowly avoided his next attack, his fist grazing past her stomach. As he stumbled past her, she seized the opportunity to land a powerful left hook to the side of his head, followed by a massive right to his jaw. Stepping back, she took a moment to assess the damage she had inflicted.

Kiara's hands reach down and grab him by the collar. She watched herself dragging the UNC caller into the bush and beat him down to the grass, the dirt, and the fallen tree branches. Her fists clutter his face, and she puts a hole in his stomach.

The man cried and begged. His voice twitches. "Don't kill me, don't kill me…"

She saw his eyes and made sure not to meet them, and she put her fist onto his nose to eliminate any vision he might have had. He was hurt, but she kept going. She needed to make sure he couldn't move by the time she was done with him.

YOU KILLED MY SON!!!

For what could I do? I had lost everything, all of myself, all, irremediably.

She took out a pistol from her jacket and shot him thrice. In that split second, time seemed to stand still, the world around her fading into a blur as she focused all her energy on the task at hand.

After all that happened in Mexico, Kiara needed some time to think. She stayed there for two days, walking around and trying to understand everything. Mexico City's colorful streets and warm sun helped her feel a bit better.

But she knew she couldn't stay there forever. There were things she needed to do back in Miami. So, she booked a flight and came back home.

Chapter 9
Betrayal

As the afternoon sun cast long shadows across the Miami streets, Jason's phone buzzed with a notification. Glancing down at the screen, he saw a message from his childhood friend Brock. A smile tugged at the corners of his lips as he read the text; Brock sounded serious.

"Hey, man. Can you meet up? Need to talk, it's really urgent."

Without hesitation, Jason typed out a quick reply. "Sure thing, Brock. Where do you want to meet?"

Brock's response came almost instantly. "How about our old spot by the river?"

"Yes, see you there around 7:00 p.m."

"Okay, I will be there," Jason said. Brock replied.

After Brock's strange message, Jason couldn't stop worrying. He went back to work, but he couldn't focus. He kept thinking about what might be wrong with his friend. Jason hoped it wasn't anything too bad.

He took a break and called his wife, Erica. He told her about meeting Brock later and that he might come home late.

"Hey, Erica. It's me. Listen, Brock just texted me. He wants to meet up. It might take a while, so I'll be a bit late getting home."

"No problem, Jason."

"Okay. I love you." Erica said.

"I love you too, honey," Jason replied.

Jason left to meet Brock as planned. He found a table and sat down, feeling a bit anxious as he waited for his best friend. After about 10 minutes of anticipation, Brock finally arrived at the meeting spot.

"Hey, Jason. Thanks for coming, man. I really appreciate it."

"No problem, Brock. You sounded serious in your text. Everything okay?"

"It's about Brent."

Jason's heart skipped a beat at the mention of his little brother's name. "What about Brent?" he asked, his voice tinged with concern.

"I found out some messed up stuff, man. It's

gonna blow your mind," Brock replied, his eyes intense with emotion. "What I'm about to tell you is listen to it carefully, and you have to get it alone."

Jason's brows furrowed in confusion. "What are you talking about, Brock? What do you mean you had to get me alone?"

Brock glanced around nervously before leaning in closer, lowering his voice. "Away from your mother, your wife, and especially Brent's dad," he explained cryptically.

Jason's heart began to race with worry. "What the hell are you saying, Brock?" he demanded. "What are you trying to tell me about my little brother?"

Brock sighed heavily; his eyes filled with sorrow. "You know Brent was like a little brother to me, too, man. I miss him so much, Jason. You know I miss him like crazy," he confessed, his voice cracking with emotion. "He was about to go to the NBA, a superstar baller..."

Jason felt a lump form in his throat as he listened to Brock's words. "Brock, please," he pleaded, his voice barely above a whisper. "Just tell me. What are you trying to tell me about Brent?"

"Man, the streets are talking, and so are the jails about Brent... about who killed Brent."

"Brock, what are you talking about, man? Who killed my baby brother?" Jason asked.

Jason's hand slams down on the table with a forceful bang.

"Romano, Erica, and your mom... they had something to do with Brent's death."

"Wait, wait...are you mad? My wife Erica, and my mom?"

"Yes, Jason. Your wife and your mom. I swear, Jason, hear me out, friend. You know I would never lie to you, man. We've been friends since second grade."

"Brock, what the hell are you saying about my wife and mom? You better talk, and I mean talk slow and tell me everything, Brock. Start talking now, man. Now!"

Jason's face is filled with terror as he awaits Brock's response.

"Wait, wait... Jason, let me explain. So, what happened was Brock was selling drugs on the college campus for Mr. Romano and his cartel."

"Wait, Brent was a drug dealer? What are you saying, man." Jason asked astonishingly.

"Let me tell you more, man. Jay, his best friend, stole all the drugs and his car. No one knows where Jay is."

"What!!! Are you even in your senses?" Jason said aggressively this time.

"Yes, I'm telling you the truth," Brock said.

"No wonder he wasn't at the funeral... I thought he was heartbroken; he blamed my little brother."

"But it's not true, Jason. There's more."

"Brock, tell me more. Please, man, I need to know."

Brock takes a deep breath, his voice trembling, and begins, "Romano, your mother's fiancé, called the hit. Brent tried to tell them that Jay had stolen the money and drugs, but they didn't believe him. One of them shot him in the head... twice. They were both pallbearers at the funeral."

"Did you know this before the funeral, Brock?"

"No, Jason, I swear. I didn't know, man. I swear." Brock said.

Jason's eyes fill with tears as he struggles to process the information.

"How is my wife involved in this, Brock? Tell me!"

"I hate to tell you this, man... Erica and Jay are having an affair. They set this whole thing up, Jason. I'm not lying. And there's more... that baby Erica's carrying? It's not yours. I have pictures, Jason. Erica and Jay have been having an affair behind your back for about two years."

Jason's world shatters as he absorbs Brock's words, his heart heavy with betrayal and pain.

"Wait, what! I'm going to kill her!" Jason responded furiously.

"No, you can't," Brock said.

The weight of Brock's revelations hits Jason like a ton of bricks, leaving him reeling with a mixture of anger, betrayal, and grief.

Brock's fingers flew across the keyboard, pulling up incriminating photos with a practiced ease. He glanced over his shoulder, meeting Jay's impatient gaze.

"Relax, man. I got 'em," Brock said, a smirk playing on his lips.

Jay's frustration boiled over. "How did you get those pics, Brock? I saw you creeping, and I was around. You took the pic?"

Brock shrugged nonchalantly. "Yeah, I snapped 'em. What's the big deal? Let me know if you want 'em."

"Send the pic, Brock. Jason needs to see it now,"

Jay demanded, his tone urgent.

"Alright, alright," Brock muttered, tapping away on his phone. "Here it is."

Jason's eyes widened as he examined the photo. "Damn it. Erica's pregnant, man. You can't do anything to her. You're gonna end up in jail."

"I don't care," Jason snapped back. "Just send the pic now, okay? We need to handle this."

"Brent was pulling in so much money. You have no idea." Brock mentioned, his voice tinged with envy. "And they were investigating Brent before he got killed."

After listening to what Brock said, Jason felt very sad. He looked down, feeling heavy and tired. Memories of things that hurt him and memories of things that were special flooded his mind, making him feel like he was drowning in sadness.

KIARA'S OFFICE

●●●

Kiara was at her desk, where everyone was working. But she wasn't thinking about her job. She felt really sad about her son and Carol. She loved Carol a lot. She couldn't focus on her work because she kept thinking about the man she loved. He was somehow involved in her son's death. She felt like she couldn't see clearly because of her love for him.

Before, love made her happy. But now it felt like something bad. She trusted him, but he hurt her. Kiara felt a surge of anger towards Mr. Romano, fueled by the pain and betrayal she had experienced. Thoughts of revenge flashed through her mind, and for a moment, the idea of ending his life seemed like the only way to ease her suffering.

But as quickly as the thought arose, Kiara pushed it away. She couldn't bring herself to seriously consider such a violent act. Despite her overwhelming emotions, she knew deep down that taking his life was not the answer.

She felt sorry for loving him. She couldn't stop feeling sad about what happened. Kiara looked at her laptop, but she couldn't concentrate. She wondered how she could ever feel better after going through so much pain. It felt like all her sadness was too heavy for her to carry like she was lost in a big ocean of sadness.

Chapter 10
The Guilt

Jason's face contorted with terror as Brock began to disclose the shocking truth.

"Jason, listen to me," Brock pleaded, his voice tinged with urgency. "I know what happened. I've been keeping quiet, but you need to know the truth. I know it's hard to accept the reality, Jason, but you have to. There's no choice."

"Tell me about my mom; how is she involved? You know that my mother is a high-profile Federal Judge. She's being approached by the FBI to help them investigate several cases because she's really good at her job. Not only this but she has been nominated by the president of the United States for the highest court in the USA. She believes in justice and equality for everyone. I don't understand how come she can be involved in such a ridiculous act." Jason said.

"I truly understand everything, Jason. But unfortunately, your mother had been engaged to Mr. Romano. She had been in love with the man who made her life worse. He's the master planner behind the drug cartel organization." Brock explains this to Jason.

"Oh my God, Brock," Jason gasped, struggling to comprehend the enormity of the betrayal. "Brock, do you know who Romano's family is?"

Brock nodded solemnly. "Yes, he's the wanted Mexican criminal who had been on the wanted list for a very long time. Jason, you need to be careful. They're dangerous people."

"I don't understand why my mother did this?" Jason said with a saddened face.

"Mr. Romano is the highest member of the drug cartel and has a lot of money and a luxurious life. Any woman can fall for that guy. Jason, I am 100% sure they have killed so many people, and your mom killed her friend and co-worker, Carol Hidding."

"WHAT!!!" Jason exclaimed.

"She put poison in her coffee. Brent and your mother knew something. Your mother, Judge Kiara Tierson, knew the whole operation." Brock said.

"I'm going to Brent's father with all this," Jason said.

"No, you can't. Mr. Madders is a great man and very heartbroken about his child getting killed. This is going to break him even more, Jason." Brock protested, desperation in his voice. "We're dealing with the Cartel here. They won't hesitate to kill anyone who gets in their way."

As Brock told Jason more stuff, Jason got more and more shocked. He couldn't believe what he was hearing.

"Brock, we have to stop them to save our lives and everyone else's," Jason suggested.

"Yes, you are right, Jason; we should do something, but what about your mother?" Brock asked curiously.

"I will deal with her and Mr. Romano one by one. Then, my wife Erica played the dirtiest game with me. I loved her so much and tried giving her everything, but what did she do to me? I hate that b*tch now and her boyfriend, Jay. I have the proof she is cheating on me and my mom. I had to get proof that she had something to do with Brent's murder. This is crazy, and I can't believe this.

I'm in shock over all this; they were at Brent's funeral like nothing happened. They are cold-blooded killers. They killed my brother. Jay and Erica set my brother up for this death trap. Where's Jay now?"

"No one knows, man, nobody knows he stole Brent's life," Brock said.

"Brock, how much did Jay steal? Do you have an idea?" Jason asked.

"I don't know, but I heard it was millions and lots of drugs," Brock replied.

"That's why Erica chose to leave me; I can't give her millions. I only make six figures, and she wanted Herme's bags of Van Cleef & Arpels jewelry. You know Brock, she has been changing. I thought it was the pregnancy, and I didn't think anything other than that, but she had been having an affair with someone else. Wow!!!! That bitch got my brother killed because she wanted a certain lifestyle, and I couldn't give that to her. I will divorce Erica."

"I feel bad for you, man," Brock said sympathetically.

Jason's heart sank as he contemplated Brock's words. "Wow... I don't think I could bring myself to hurt her or the baby, even if it's not mine. I still love her despite everything she did to me."

Jason sat there for a while with Brock. He was really sad and felt alone.

"I can't tell you, Brock, how alone I have been feeling now," Jason said while crying.

Brock took Jason's hand and tried to console him. "Everything will be okay, Jason," Brock said.

KIARA'S HOME

●●●

Kiara finally arrived back home, her body heavy with exhaustion and sadness. After a long shower, she slipped into comfortable clothes, her mind numb with fatigue. All she wanted was to collapse onto her bed and drift into a deep sleep. The weight of her grief pressed down on her, and she longed for the days when Brent was alive, and Mr. Romano hadn't entered her life. Tears streamed down her cheeks as she yearned to reclaim the simplicity of her past.

As Kiara lay on her bed, lost in thoughts of her former life, her phone suddenly rang. With a heavy sigh, she picked it up to see Jason's name flashing on the screen.

"Hey, Mom?" Jason's voice came through the phone.

Kiara's heart warmed at the sound of her son's voice. "Hello, Jason, my sweet boy. How's everything?" she replied, her tone filled with motherly concern.

"I'm doing really well, Mom," Jason responded. "And how about you?"

"Oh, sweetheart, I've been managing," Kiara replied.

"That's great to hear! Can we meet, Mom?" Jason asked eagerly.

Kiara's brow furrowed slightly with curiosity. "Of course, honey. What's on your mind? Is everything alright with you?"

"Yes, Mom, everything's fine. I just... I just wanted to see you. Can we meet somewhere outside of the house?" Jason requested tentatively.

"Yes, of course, Jason. Whatever you need. I'm at home, but we can meet elsewhere."

"Umm... can we meet somewhere else?" Jason asked.

"Absolutely, that sounds lovely," Kiara agreed, her

heart fluttering with anticipation.

"Okay, Mom, I'll text you the details," Jason said.

"Alright, Jason," Kiara replied, her voice soft with affection.

After they hung up, Jason quickly sent her the location and time, eager to reconnect with his mother.

At the Matheson Hammock Park around 7 p.m.

Jason took a deep breath as he dialed Mr. Romano's number. After a moment of ringing, Romano picked up.

"Mr. Romano, it's Jason. Can we meet?" Jason asked.

"Yeah, sure, what's up, Jason?" Romano replied casually.

"Nothing just wanted to spend some time with you," Jason said, trying to keep his tone nonchalant.

There was a brief pause before Romano responded, "Of course, Jason."

"That's great, Mr. Romano. I'll text you the location and time," Jason said.

"Okay, see you soon, Jason," Romano replied before they hung up.

After ending the call, Jason quickly sent Romano a text message:

Matheson Hammock Park around 7 p.m.

As the evening approached, Jason braced himself for the meeting ahead. At 7 p.m., Kiara arrived at the park to find Jason already waiting for her.

"Jason," Kiara greeted him with a small smile as she approached.

"Mom, nice to see you," Jason replied.

They stood facing each other, the quiet of the park surrounding them.

"I'm glad you're here," Jason began, his voice tinged with uncertainty.

Kiara reached out, placing a hand on his arm. "I'm always here for you, Jason. What's on your mind?"

Jason took a deep breath, gathering his thoughts. "I've been thinking a lot lately... about everything that's happened."

Kiara nodded, her eyes reflecting understanding. "It's been a lot to process. But you don't have to face it alone."

"I know," Jason said while, his gaze drifting away momentarily before returning to meet his mother's eyes.

"I just... I need to figure things out with everything. With you and with everyone else, too."

"What do you mean, Jason?" Kiara asked, curiosity lacing her words.

"You will get to know that, Mom," Jason replied cryptically, a mischievous grin playing on his lips.

Before their conversation could delve any deeper, Mr. Romano was already there. Kiara's expression shifted subtly, her demeanor becoming more guarded as she observed Romano's approach. "What are you doing here?" she asked Mr. Romano angrily.

Mr. Romano approached them with a calm demeanor, his eyes meeting Kiara's with a steady gaze. "Jason called me here to talk about something."

Kiara glanced between Jason and Mr. Romano; her uncertainty evident. "Talk about what, exactly? Jason does want to talk to you. Leave my family alone."

Jason stepped forward, his expression resolute, and yelled. "Stop, both of you. You made everything worse. Stop this drama now."

"WHAT! Jason, what are you talking about, honey?" Kiara's voice quivered with shock and disbelief.

"Stop this, Mom, please! Enough of your

innocence," Jason retorted, his tone filled with frustration and anger.

Kiara turned towards Mr. Romano, her eyes blazing with fury. "It's all because of you. You have made my life a living hell."

"What did I do to you, Kiara?" Mr. Romano's voice held a note of confusion.

"What did you do? Stop pretending that everything is fine when it's not," Kiara exclaimed, her voice rising with each word.

As the argument escalated between Kiara and Mr. Romano, Jason's heart pounded in his chest. He knew what he had to do. With a trembling hand, he reached into his pocket and pulled out a gun.

"I'm sorry, both of you, but you don't deserve to live now," Jason whispered, his voice trembling with emotion.

Without hesitation, he aimed the gun and fired, the sound echoing through the quiet park. Kiara and Mr. Romano fell to the ground, their lifeless bodies lying motionless amidst the bloodstained grass.

Tears streamed down Jason's cheeks as he stood there, his mind consumed by turmoil. He screamed into the empty night, "Rest in Paradise, Little Brother. Love You."

With a final act of desperation, Jason turned the gun on himself and pulled the trigger. The sound reverberated through the stillness of the park as his body collapsed beside his mother and Mr. Romano.

All three of them lay there, their blood mingling with the earth, their lives tragically intertwined in a moment of unspeak.

Epilogue

There was darkness everywhere. It was a pitch-black night with no moon in the sky. There was just a dim glow of the streetlights.

Jay approached Erica's house. It was big and lavish but looked scariest now. There was a dreadful silence. He went inside and came back with two suitcases in both of his hands.

Without saying a word, Jay and Erica both sat in a car. She slipped into the passenger seat beside him, and her expression was unreadable.

Erica glanced out of the corner of her eye to her home but didn't say a word. Then, she looked at Jay for a while. This is my life; Jay is my true love.

They both sat quietly, not saying anything, lost in some thoughts. Jay ignited the engine, nodded at Erica, and started looking ahead again and they drove away.

It's better that everyone's dead than alive,
Give me what I asked for – for my good, not yours,
This is what I wanted – my eyes just upon myself,
Life, at his death, a memory without guilt!

www.ingramcontent.com/pod-product-compliance
Lightning Source LLC
Chambersburg PA
CBHW040823010826
48978CB00012BB/594